Tam knew her relationship with Stewart was too good to be true.

What's wrong, she wondered, and then she knew this was the night the party would end. He was trying to find a kind way to tell her he was not going to take her out any more, that the romance was over but that they could remain friends. He was trying not to hurt her feelings.

Well, all right, she could cope with that. She'd been expecting it. She'd make it easy for both of them. She'd thank him for all the fun and they would part friends.

"Tam," he began, and she braced herself as he looked straight at her, "Tam, I. . .Oh, I'm not very good at this."

Releasing her hand, he dug in his blazer pocket and fumbled out a little square box. "Open it," he said.

Inside, glittering against blue velvet, was a breathtaking diamond ring.

"Will you marry me, Tam?" He took the ring from the box and slipped it on her finger, where it glittered in the moonlight.

"It's beautiful," she breathed.

"So are you," he whispered. "You and I can have a good life together."

She fluttered her fingers slowly, watching the moonlight play on the diamond. It dazzled her. Moonlight, handsome man, diamond—a dream, perfect. Almost.

JANET GORTSEMA lives in Pleasantville, New York with her husband, Frank, and is an English teacher at Sleepy Hollow High School. *Design for Love* marks her debut as a *Heartsong Presents* author.

Design
for Love

Janet Gortsema

Heartsong Presents

To Frank, with love and gratitude.

ISBN 1-55748-434-1

DESIGN FOR LOVE

one

From her perch on the edge of the loading platform, Tam could get a breath of air, eat a quick supper, and relax for a few minutes with Vickie and Barbara. And Hope, of course.

Here at the Food Mart they all did the same kind of work and Hope did her share, but Hope was different. She had "college" written all over her. In just a few years she'd be on her way to the beautiful life Tam used to dream of.

When Tam was sixteen, her mother was alive and her father was still top salesman for Archetype Office Supplies. Tam planned to study art in college, maybe finish in Paris. Then she'd be a commercial artist or, probably, an interior decorator. She loved to work with beautiful things.

She'd always had a way with color and design and could draw well enough to put her ideas on paper. She could see, in her mind, exactly how a room would look, even before the decorating was started. She thought she could have been a good decorator.

Now, at twenty-seven, the only artwork Tam did was painting occasional sale signs or setting up a fancy display of catfood.

Barb and Vickie teased her about being arty, but they teased gently. Tam was as stuck in Food Mart as they were, so they forgave her for dreaming.

They didn't forgive Hope for being lovely and for

coasting through their lives on her way to easy living. They teased Hope too, but not gently.

"What do you suppose Hopeless is looking for in the garbage?" snickered Barbara. The acid in Barb's voice said Barb wasn't really asking what Hope was doing, but was inviting Tam and Vickie to join in her favorite game of badgering Hope.

Just off the far end of the platform the target of Barb's game was tossing aside citrus wrappers and pushing away boxes, her slim young figure and satiny blond hair as foreign in the rubbish pile as caviar in oatmeal.

Tam sighed. She disliked this game and tried to avoid it whenever possible, but she knew she had to play along if she wanted to keep peace with Barb and Vickie. She needed these friends who worked cash registers next to her.

"She's probably hunting for a little snack," Vickie sniped. "Maybe a not-too-rotten orange to take home."

"No,' said Barb. "She's looking for more honey to put on her super-sweet personality."

Hope heard, as they intended, but she didn't respond. She kept searching.

Answer them, thought Tam. *Just once answer the way they deserve so they let you alone.* But Tam knew Hope couldn't. Or wouldn't. Tam said, "What are you looking for?"

Hope straightened. "I thought I heard a noise, a soft cry like a kitten. I don't hear it now. It must be gone."

"Careful, Hope," warned Tam. "It might be a rat."

Hope jerked her hands back.

"Maybe not," Tam went on, "but. . . ."

Hope reluctantly backed out of the trash pile.

"Maybe you just thought you heard something," said Vickie.

"Yeah, Hope," Barb said. "Maybe you imagined it, like you imagine that stuff about heaven and angels. With your connections in heaven, you should be able to imagine a kittycat into existence out of nowhere if you want to. Or a tiger. Yeah. If you imagine a cat, make it a big one. A full-sized tiger shouldn't be hard for someone with your connections."

Hope didn't answer. Tam wished Barb would stop, but once Barb started on Hope about religion, she wouldn't stop until she had worn the subject out. For Tam it was worn out already.

Enough, thought Tam. She stood, saying, "I think I hear something too—Mack yelling for us to get back to work."

"Mack can wait till I'm good and ready to come in," grouched Barb. "It's not 7:30 yet and I'm not ready."

"It's 7:30 by my watch," said Tam. "I'm going in. I need this job. You know Mack gets angry when we're late. Maybe Mack is sweet on you, so you can get by with it, but he's not in love with me. I'm going." She started toward the heavy fire door to the back storeroom.

Being teased about Mack was like candy to Barb, who reacted as Tam hoped she would. Barb would let Hope alone if she could have more teasing about Mack. She followed Tam through the door. Neither mentioned that the time clock showed only 7:27.

Talk about Mack's being sweet on Barb was only talk, of course. No one even remembered how it got started, certainly not from anything Mack said or did. As far as Tam knew, the only thing Mack cared about was his grocery. Employees were workers, nothing more. Besides, only a brave man would stand up to Barbara's dangerous comments. Tam couldn't think of a man who dared try.

Barbara wasn't so bad. Now and then something brought out that little mean streak, but mostly she was pretty good company. She could even be kind and steady, as she was when Tam's mother died. Inside, *far* inside, Barb was a softy.

If anyone had told Tam when she first took the grocery job that Vickie and Barb would be almost her only friends, she would have laughed. She laughed more readily then and had many friends. Most had gone through school together in the smallish Indiana "city" of Empton. Most went to the same church, where they learned to sing "Jesus Loves the Little Children" in Sunday school and sat on the same hard benches to listen to their pastor, Mr. Simms, on Sunday mornings and evenings. In high school they all belonged to youth group and grew even closer.

Tam cherished these memories, but at twenty-seven they seemed like someone else's life. High school was finished and most of the old gang had married, or moved away, or both. Even Robert was gone.

"Rabbit" they called him, the first kid in his class with big front teeth replacing his baby teeth. "Rabbit," until they fell in love in high school. Then he was Robert, and she was Tamara, not the "Tam" she was to everyone else.

Well, Rabbit or Robert—what difference? He was gone. He went to college; she stayed to finish her senior year, to graduate and join him at Indiana State, as planned.

Then Dad's stroke ended the plans. He never worked again. His mind tangled his speech. The clinic called it "sensory aphasia." Words no longer came out right. He might be thinking "pocket," for example, but say "shoe" or some other word that made no sense. No one knew what he would say next. Sometimes he said appalling things. *If it weren't so awful,* Tam thought, *it might be funny.*

A salesman without words is lost. He had covered most of Illinois and Indiana, his territory. Now he went nowhere but to the clinic once a week, and to the library after that.

Tam didn't go to college, not with an out-of-work father and an overworked mother. Tam and her mother had done their best to hold things together. Tam had already been working part-time at Food Mart. When she graduated, she moved to full time, working days and asking for overtime.

Her mother worked nights at Lincoln Elementary as custodial matron, scrubbing bathrooms, cleaning the main office. That and taking care of her husband had worn her out. When flu caught her two years ago, she had no strength to fight off the pneumonia that followed it.

Nothing much changed after that. Tam still cared for her father and the house. She forgot about art and decorating and a social life—all those non-essentials. She forgot about Robert, almost, which was lucky, because Robert definitely had forgotten about her.

She worked, slept, cared for her father, worked, slept— round the circle of her days, day after day, night-shift after night-shift. (Nights pay a little more.)

She wasn't unhappy. Or happy. She was numb, going through the motions of living without having a life.

If she had looked, she might have found more friends, perhaps even a new man. He wouldn't have replaced Robert, but he'd have been someone to share with, maybe even to love.

She didn't look.

The only men she knew well were the ones at work—gangling teens and men not interested in a drab leftover in her late twenties. (Well, middle twenties, but it felt late.) She didn't blame them.

At work she wore the company smock over old cotton skirts and blouses, summer or winter, glad to save clothing money for things needed at home. She told herself she had better things to do than keep her hair curly and her clothes smooth.

She'd changed since she was a black-haired, blue-eyed, willowy teenager. Her eyes were still deep blue, but they no longer sparkled. Her hair was still black, most of it, but she could see traces of white. She solved that problems by not looking. When she didn't tie it up out of the way, her hair still hung long, but it had no more life than her laughter. She had almost stopped laughing.

Almost. Sometimes at work things were so crazy she just had to laugh. Vickie and Barb joked through the hours at the registers, making the night short and light.

Barbara survives by laughing, Tam thought. Barb was about Tam's age, but had a little daughter. Barb had never been married and her life was not easy, even with her sister's help.

Vickie was different. Younger, she still lived at home and probably always would. Learning was difficult and she felt lucky to have a job she could handle. She knew she still would have been sweeping up if Barb and Tam hadn't spent hours teaching her to operate the register. Luckily the machine figured correct change, so Vickie could manage.

Vickie was first to punch in every day, glad to be there, anxious to put her fingers to the numbered keys, to call out the prices proudly.

Vickie followed Barb and Tam back to those registers from the supper break. That's the way it was. Barb was the leader, Vickie the follower, and Tam neither.

They still had a minute left when Tam replaced Mack at the register. He looked at the clock and then at her, puzzled, but she merely shrugged. He didn't need to hear why she had hurried to end the dinner entertainment.

Next in line was Mr. Brill. He came in often, usually for one or two items. The "girls" always asked if he had forgotten anything. Mr. Brill always said, "Whatever it is, I'll get it next time." It was ritual. Next time would be tomorrow, or the next day, at the latest.

"Only bread tonight, Mr. Brill?" Tam asked. "What did you forget?"

"Whatever it is, I'll get it next time," he said. "I only come in here to see you good-looking girls."

He said things like that and they played along. "Sure," Tam answered. "You come in here to see our beautiful smiling faces. Right?"

"Right. Where else can I talk to such girls?"

Barbara called from her register one, "Come through my line next time, Mr. Brill. You always get in Tam's line. You never talk to me any more."

"Tam's my favorite," he called back, winking broadly at Tam.

Barb knew it was only talk and called, "All right for you, Mr. Brill. If you don't love me anymore, I'll get a new boyfriend."

He laughed, lapping up the attention. "Don't I get carry-out service?"

"For one little loaf of bread? With all your muscles, you

should be able to manage with no trouble at all," teased Tam, bagging his rye with caraway seeds. "Shall I call Al to carry it out for you?"

"Never mind; I'll struggle along by myself." He picked up the bag with one hand. "See you next time." He winked again and was gone.

"Tam's got an admirer," laughed Barb.

"You're just jealous," answered Tam, because she knew it was nonsense. "Besides, a girl could do worse. He can't be much over fifty, not bad looking, and still has his own teeth. Must have, if he buys bread with seeds in it."

"Listen to her, Vickie. She's inspecting his teeth now. This girl gets right to the important stuff."

They passed the hours talking of one thing and another. Some regular customers came in and there were the usual quiet spots between rushes. When not up front, they helped with pricing and shelving or with returning "orphans," items shoppers abandoned in the wrong places: a tomato in the soap section, milk with the frozen juice, bread perched on the eggs. Keeping busy made the time go faster and kept Mack happy. The stock boys appreciated the help too and returned the favor by bagging at checkout.

Quitting time came fast enough. At eleven the girls went back to hang up their smocks and punch out.

They had worked there so long that each had several smocks. Some were badly worn, kept only for emergencies like the time a big bottle of grape of soda exploded all over Vickie.

As Tam reached up to hang her smock on the hook, Barb said, "Better take yours home tonight, Tam. Looks like it needs washing."

"I just washed—"

Barb cut off Tam's words with a sharp elbow to her ribs. Looking quickly about, Barb pushed a large package of gum into Tam's and showed her the pocket of her own smock. It held more gum packages. "Better take your smock home tonight," she said. "Vickie and I are."

Tam put the gum back in Barb's hand. "Not tonight. It's clean enough."

Barb shrugged and dropped the gum into her pocket, folding the smock over her arm to hide the bulge. "Watch it," she warned, not quite in fun; "You'll get as pure as Hopeless over there." She jerked her head toward the corner where Hope was hanging up her smock.

"No chance," said Tam.

Barb grinned and nodded, friendly again. "See ya."

"See ya, Barb. See ya, Vickie." Tam loitered a bit on fake business to avoid walking out with Barb and that pocketful of gum. Barb took things now and then, little things. Tam objected, but Barb always argued that the store wouldn't miss a few inexpensive items and that the little bit Mack paid wasn't enough. She felt he owed her a candy bar or a package of gum if she wanted it. It wasn't as if she stole cash from the register, was it?

Tam felt oddly guilty, though she hadn't accepted the gum. Telling Mack would cause trouble and it didn't seem worth taking a chance on getting fired over a silly package of gum or two. Still, Tam was uncomfortable with it.

"I'll walk out with you," Hope offered. They took their time cards from the rack and, Tam first, pushed them into the slot of the time clock far enough to trigger the old-fashioned stamping mechanism. Seven minutes after eleven. They went through the swinging door next to produce and walked past packaged meats and down frozens to checkout and then out the front door.

After eight, Mack wanted those back doors locked and bolted and no one was allowed to go out that way. Tam was glad to comply. At night the loading platform was much less friendly looking than it was in the daylight, even with two big spotlights on. She felt better going out the front door into a parking lot with cars and people in it.

At the edge of the lot, where their pathways divided, Hope said, "You were right."

"About what?" Tam asked.

"About the gum," Hope said. "You were right about not taking it. She's going to get herself fired one of these times."

Tam snapped to attention. "How did you know?"

Hope said, "Everybody knows."

"Are you going to tell Mack?" asked Tam.

Hope considered. "I don't think so. No. Anyway, I think he already knows. He just hasn't said anything yet. If she stops now, maybe he never will say anything. I'd try to get her to stop before she gets fired, but she wouldn't listen to me. She'll listen to you, though."

Tam shook her head. "I don't know about that. Barbara does what she wants to do. If I tell her not to take things, she might take something bigger just to show me she can do as she pleases. Besides, why should you care what happens to her? She's not exactly gentle with you. How do I know you're not trying to break up our friendship to get even with her for all the hard times she gives you?"

Hope smiled. "You don't know. You'll simply have to make up your own mind whether or not you can trust me. Think about it. Think about your friend Barbara, too, and what will happen to her if Mack fires her. Then do what you think is right."

"You have more confidence in me than I have," Tam mumbled.

"Yes, I do, said Hope. "I have a lot of confidence in you. See you tomorrow."

"Yeah," Tam said, and turned to the left without looking back.

Strange girl, that Hope, she thought. Tam's steps lengthened as she swung into the rhythm of the long walk home. She headed toward the center of town where the streets were lighter than they were on the shortcut through the side streets.

On the way to work in daylight, Tam usually took the shortcut. She'd walked the side streets so often that she had come to know some of the people along the way; not by name, of course, but well enough to nod to and exchange greetings. In the dark, though, she went out of her way to take the brighter streets across one end of the main part of town.

At sixteen she had been afraid on the dark streets alone at night. At first, Robert had taken care of her, meeting her after work and riding her home on his motorcycle. Once or twice, after he had gone, she had tried waiting for the bus. It was a long, dark wait at eleven o'clock. Better to keep moving if she had to be out there alone. It might not be safer, but it felt safer.

Two short blocks led to the bright lights, then eight long blocks through town before the five unavoidable dark blocks through neighborhood streets. She knew it by heart and strode home night after night without thinking where to turn. Her father used to say that his car knew the way home by itself, like an old horse. So did Tam's feet.

Sometime she ought to add up all the blocks she had walked in the last eleven years. It must be hundreds, maybe thousands. While she walked, she thought, doing most of her private thinking in the night streets.

That night she thought about Hope. Strange girl. Hope must be so tired of Barb's unending sarcasm that she would be glad of a chance to get even, to give Barb a little slap, kind of. Maybe that's what Hope wanted. Maybe she thought she could use Tam to get at Barbara. Maybe Hope thought she could break up the three friends.

She ought to know better. They'd been friends too long for that.

Hope sounded concerned over Barb's losing her job. What would Hope know about that? To Barb and Tam that job was food on the table. Without it they'd be in big trouble. But Hope didn't have to support anybody else. If the job blew up she could go back to her books. In another year or so she wouldn't need Food Mart. She'd be living one of those lives Tam used to dream about. What difference did it make to Hope what happened to Barbara?

On the other hand, in the whole year and a half that Tam had known her, Hope had never given any reason not to trust her. In fact, only yesterday she could have blamed the broken bottle of ammonia in aisle four on Tam, but she hadn't. Hope was out of aisle four before the ammonia smell got to the front where Mack noticed it. When the fumes hit his nose, Tam was right there at the end of that aisle. Hope didn't have to tell him she knocked it off the shelf. When she did tell him, she could have pointed out that she knocked it off because Al had shelved it too close to the front edge. She didn't say that. She said she knocked it off and was sorry and would clean it up right away.

That's all. Al helped her, which was only fair.

If she really wanted to get even with Barb, she had had plenty of chances. Yet she never answered Barbara the way Barbara spoke to her. Never. Even when Barb sneered about her religion.

Hope was too smart to think she could get at Barb through Tam, and Tam couldn't imagine her doing something just for spite. There was no spite in her.

Maybe, thought Tam, *Hope really cares what happens to Barbara.* She might be right about Mack's knowing what was going on. Hope said she wouldn't tell and Tam believed her.

Hope could be right about the rest of it too. If Barb would listen to anyone, that person would be Tam.

I'd rather stay out of it, Tam thought. But as Barb's friend she was already involved. Tam might be able to convince her. After all, Hope said she had confidence in Tam. Tam was surprised how good that made her feel. She would try.

Five blocks from the parking lot, a long green car pulled up to the curb next to her. She saw it out of the corner of her eye, but she didn't turn. She had read somewhere that women walking alone at night should look as if they knew where they were going and should move purposefully ahead, not making eye contact with strangers. She hurried purposefully ahead.

"Tam? Is that you, Tam?"

At the sound of the familiar voice she turned to look at the car cruising slowly along the edge of the road, staying even with her. She stopped.

"Mr. Brill?" She peered at the face behind the passenger's window. She could see him stretching across as far as he could to speak to her through the open window. "Is that you, Mr. Brill?"

"It's me all right, Tam. Want a ride?'

"No, thanks. I like to walk."

"Are you sure? It's no trouble. I'm going this direction anyway."

"No thanks. I need the exercise." She started walking again.

He waved and she waved back. Then he drove on down the street, gave the horn a little beep at next corner, and turned left.

She felt silly then. It was a long walk home and she was tired. She wished she'd taken the ride. He'd caught her off-guard and she wasn't thinking fast. After all those nights of walking in the scary dark and hoping no one would notice her, she was simply not ready to hop in the car with the first person who offered a lift, even though she knew him.

Silly, she thought. *I wish I'd taken the ride.*

two

At almost midnight Tam opened the side door of her house on Terhune Street. It was dark, with no light at all except the light in the attic next door.

Tam gazed up at the light. Mrs. Warren was usually asleep by this time, worn out from cleaning. She was the cleanest person in the neighborhood, maybe the whole town. If it stood still, she cleaned it. She even took those little plastic plates off the wall, the ones behind the light switches, and cleaned behind them. Tam decided she must still be up hunting for dust.

Nevertheless, midnight was way past Mrs. Warren's usual bedtime. She might have gotten into one of her famous disasters, like the time she tried to wash the ceiling over the basement stairs and fell of the wobbly board she was balancing on. She'd broken an arm and was lucky, at that. Tam had heard the crash and come running to rescue her.

Mrs. Warren, Tam's mother's best friend, had lived next door since before Tam was born. Her children were older than Tam, big kids when Tam was little, and had homes of their own now. Mrs. Warren was left alone in her spotless, empty house.

I'd better check, thought Tam.

She crunched onto the gravel driveway between the two houses, around the back of a beat-up, no-color van parked there. Van? Mrs. Warren didn't have a van. Her little sky-blue sedan was doubtless tucked neatly away in her spotless garage. Company? No. The kitchen would be lit, and probably the living room. Tam had to know if Mrs. Warren was all right.

From the middle of the drive, behind that strange van, Tam whispered loudly up to the open attic window, "Mrs. Warren?" Silence. She called again, more loudly. Silence.

She found a piece of gravel and threw it lightly against the screen. "Mrs. Warren?" As her second stone hit the screen dead center, a face appeared in the window. A man's face.

"What do you want?" the stranger growled.

"Where's Mrs. Warren?"

"In bed, of course," the man answered. "Why?"

Tam ignored his question, demanding, "Who are you? Why are you in Mrs. Warren's attic?"

"I'm Luke and I live here. Okay?"

It was definitely not okay. Tam yelled, "Mrs. Warren?"

"Here I am, dear," said Mrs. Warren's voice from close by. The kitchen light came on, illuminating her neighbor's face at the kitchen window. "I'm all right, dear. Just fine. You go in now."

"But. . ."

"It's all right, Tam. Really. I'll explain tomorrow. Now stop upsetting the neighborhood. Good night." She left the window and the kitchen was dark again.

Tam looked up at the silhouette in the attic window. He didn't speak, didn't move.

Weird, she thought, waiting another second or two before turning away. She let herself in her own side door and from behind the curtain watched the face watch her door. The face vanished. Weird. What had Mrs. Warren gotten into this time?

By the glow of the kitchen nightlight, Tam put the tea kettle on as she did every night and went to see if her father was awake. She knew he would be; he always was. As usual she pretended to think he was asleep alone in the house.

"Dad," she whispered at the door of his room, "Are you awake?"

"No," he said. He wasn't trying to be funny. "No" was one of those favorite words he said whenever he couldn't say the word he wanted.

"Good," said Tam, knowing exactly what he meant. "I'm having a cup of tea. Would you like one?"

"No," he said. "I'll get the cups."

Every night they sat together at the kitchen table, sharing tea and the news of the day. Mostly, Tam talked and he listened, but sometimes in the relaxed quiet of the night he tried to say things.

She listened for the meaning behind his words and didn't correct him when he said something silly or empty. She might repeat what she thought he meant and ask if that was right, but she was careful not to sound critical.

That half hour in the middle of the night was important to both of them. They savored the closeness before she tucked him in for the night. When Tam was little, she never felt officially in bed until she'd been tucked in by her mother. Now she tucked her father in.

As she turned off the kitchen light, a car pulled into Mrs. Warren's driveway. From the window she could see the zippy little sports car park behind the van. A man got out and went into the side door directly across from Tam.

She followed his progress through the house by the lights

he turned on and off. He went to Billy's room and stayed there. Now what? She could hardly wait to see Mrs. Warren in the morning.

She locked up and went to bed in the little room between the kitchen and Dad's room, the room she'd slept in all her life. Breezes from the open window were cool across the foot of the bed, so she put her pillow at that end and lay wrong way, enjoying the air.

Billy's room was still bright. So was the attic.

When she woke, both cars were gone and laundry was already hanging in the backyard. Clattering dishes told her Dad was in the kitchen. The therapist insisted Dad wasn't to be babied; he was to carry whatever part of the work he could manage. Dad could manage breakfast, so it was his job to make tea and toast for Tam and orange juice and hot cereal for himself.

Occasionally Tam thought she might prefer a little variety, but changes were upsetting to him and therefore to her so she resigned herself to finding exactly the same breakfast ready every day when she came into the kitchen, dressed for the day.

Eight was about as early as she ever woke up, so nine was her usual breakfast hour. Even then she was not wide awake and cheery like those peculiar people on television commercials whose chief joy in life is cereal.

Dad, however, woke with the birds. He loved the birds. First thing every morning, winter or summer, he went to the back window to see which of "his" birds were out there. He knew them all by name and habit because he'd looked them up in the bird book he kept handy on table. He'd borrowed it from the library so often that Tam had given him a copy for his birthday.

This interest was an outgrowth of the therapy sessions, "lessons" that had been regular practice with Tam and her dad ever since his release from the hospital. He'd flatly refused to work with her mother, perhaps out of pride, so Tam had tried. In the beginning, it was difficult for both of them. She didn't know what to do and he didn't want to cooperate. Gradually it got easier. He grew accustomed to learning from his own child and she grew more confident. They settled into a prolonged experiment in communication.

The clinic's speech therapist told Tam what to do and let her watch Dad's Tuesday morning therapy sessions. At home Tam tried to copy what the therapist had done, with minor variations to keep Dad interested. That's how they got involved with birds.

Tuesdays, Mrs. Warren lent them her car to go to the clinic. To prolong the luxury of having their own transportation, they had developed the habit of stopping at the library on their way home. It made the morning fuller, richer, and Mrs. Warren didn't mind.

Dad would browse, sometimes in the reference section, randomly opening dusty atlases or encyclopedias, turning pages until he found an item that caught his interest. Then he'd take his volume and settle in the large window seat until time to go.

Meanwhile, Tam looked for something interesting to take home for those lessons. First she tried sports books, especially baseball. After months of batting statistics and World Series records, they switched to travel. She'd name a place and he would try to tell her what country or state it was in. Sometimes he couldn't say it but could point to it. Other times he rattled off names of places like nothing was wrong with him. When they found places neither of them had heard of, he looked them up in the index— valuable practice in alphabetical organization, very important, according to the therapist.

After sports and geography came math, at which he was very clever. She couldn't predict what he would or wouldn't be able to do. Both were surprised that, after wrestling with the alphabet, numbers were a snap.

Tam read to him often, usually from westerns. Then she discovered he could read perfectly well by himself. She still read to him occasionally, to keep him company and break the television monotony.

He could also write, which seemed odd to her, considering the difficulty he had with talking. Writing helped when he had something to say and the words wouldn't come out.

After baseball and travel and math came birds. One day he picked up *The Audubon Society Field Guide To North American Birds, Eastern Region,* and fell in love with birds.

It took much patience on his part to pull from his memory things that any child knows and that he knew too, if only he could remember them. With frustration always just beneath the surface, he had only tenuous control of his temper.

When he shouted and stamped off to turn on the television in the middle of a lesson, Tam wished he were more easygoing. Then she reminded herself that the stubbornness kept him trying day after day, kept him getting up in the morning when there was nothing to look forward to but another "lesson" and afternoon television.

After two years of lessons the therapist took Tam aside and explained that Dad wasn't going to get better. Two years was the general rule, she said. He had improved as much as he was going to. Tam should quit trying so hard. Progress from then on would be slow indeed and probably not worth the time and effort.

Tam still got angry when she thought of the therapist telling her to quit, but now she realized that the therapist was just trying to spare Tam some heartache. Too late. Tam already had the heartache and she had no intention of giving up on her father. If he was stubborn, so was she.

Improvement came slowly now. Each rare, tiny gain was a triumph.

He was sly though. If the right word took too much effort, he took another word. Once he had a word that sounded good to him, he stayed with it until it was the easiest word, almost the only word he could think of. That June, his best word was "no."

That's what he said when Mrs. Warren stuck her head in the back door that morning. "No," he said, in greeting.

"Yes," said Mrs. Warren, and came right in with some lettuce from her garden. "You'll have to wash this. I just picked it fresh."

"Thank you," said Tam, thinking that in Mrs. Warren's garden the vegetables probably wouldn't dare get dirty. "We'll enjoy it, won't we, Dad?

"No."

"Knew you would," said Mrs. Warren, pulling a chair out and settling herself at the table. "Thought you might like to know who that man was you yelled at in the middle of the night. Can't have you calling the police on me."

Tam started to object that she was just worried, but Mrs.

Warren raised a hand to silence Tam and went on with her explanation.

"Oh, I know you were just worried, and I appreciate it. Nothing like having good neighbors to watch over you. Makes me feel real safe over there alone just knowing you folks are watching out for me. It's good to know you're here, but it's not enough. With the children married and William gone, there's nobody for me to look after.

"Too quiet, too," she went on. "I miss the noise the kids made. The radio's no good to talk to or cook for. Got to have more than that."

Tam said, "You have more than that. You're always helping somebody out. Dad and I wouldn't know what to do without you. And you teach Sunday school and belong to—"

"Bible Study and Missionary Circle," she finished for Tam. "And of course there's ceramics class on Tuesday nights. I'm busy enough. It's not that. I need somebody to care for. You understand, don't you, John?"

Tam's father nodded.

"I need somebody in the house, somebody to make noise and eat my cooking and stir up some dust. That's why I asked Stewart and Luke to live with me. Don't scowl. Tam; they're perfectly nice boys. Stewart's from Rev. Moore's old church in Ohio and Luke's his army buddy. Reverend Moore told me about them. He brought them over yesterday and they liked the house so much they checked right out of that motel.

"Moved in yesterday, if that's what you call it. Everything they had was in that old van of Luke's. They were real glad to get out of that motel, practically jumped at Billy's and Lucy's rooms. The clincher, though was my attic. Luke needs a place to work and the attic's the very thing.

"Nice to have a little activity in the house again." Mrs. Warren looked pleased with herself.

Dad cleared his throat and looked at Tam, who said what they both were thinking. "Just how old are these 'boys'?"

"A little older than you, I'd guess, Tam. About the age of my children."

Dad spoke. "Do they. . ."

They waited while he groped for the rest of the words. ". . .work?" he finished triumphantly. "Do they work?"

"Oh, yes," Mrs. Warren bubbled. "At least, Stewart does. That's why they're here. He's overseeing the opening of the new Haberson's store in the mall, the new one they're building out on the bypass. I don't know how long he'll stay, but he'll be here till it opens at least, and maybe a while after."

"What about the other one?" asked Tam. "The one who wants to work in your attic."

"Luke. He's an artist. Isn't that wonderful?" said Mrs. Warren. "Imagine being able to paint pictures right from your imagination. You would understand that, Tam. Luke has the whole attic, except for the end where I store my Christmas decorations and off-season clothes. He can paint up there as long as he likes and nobody will bother him."

Tam speculated, "He must be a very successful artist to be able to live on the income from his paintings. If he's that good, why doesn't he have a studio somewhere?"

"Well, he doesn't actually support himself with his pictures yet." Mrs. Warren said this uncertainly, as if she'd rather not say it at all. "He's out looking for a job to live on so he can devote his time to his real work. I'm sure he'll find one soon."

Mrs. Warren had made up her mind about these "boys." That was evident by the way she defended them to her friends. It was useless to try to change her mind, whatever misgivings they might have.

"I hope it turns out the way you want it to," offered Tam.

Dad said, "Hope it turns out."

"It will; don't you worry. It's going to be fine. Got to go get that cobbler baked and the mess in the driveway cleaned up in time to make those boys a decent supper. So much to do. Isn't it lovely?"

"No," said Dad, and Tam knew he meant it that time, but Mrs. Warren didn't hear him because she was gone before she had finished talking.

Tam watched her prance across the driveway and wondered vaguely where the mess was. She didn't see one. What she saw was a very happy neighbor lady who looked years younger than she had last week.

Amazing, thought Tam. *Who would believe that having someone to take care of would make her so young? It doesn't have that effect on me. What makes her so happy?*

She sighed and turned back to her father. "Just one more time through the exercise and we'll quit. "Repeat: 'Breakfast is ready.'"

"'Breakfast is ready,'" he repeated, and smiled.

"Good, Dad," she said. "Did you fix the lawn mower?"

"Did you fix the lawn mower?" he echoed.

"No, Dad, I'm asking. I want to know if you fixed the mower."

"No," he said.

She looked at the knee-high weeds in the backyard, a

shabby tangle next to Mrs. Warren's manicured green. It would take more than a mower to cut through that. It would take a haying machine.

"We could get a goat," she said, looking him straight in the eye. There was absolutely no trace of a smile on her face. "Mrs. Warren would love living next door to a goat."

He looked away. He could easily have fixed the mower and they both knew it. In a slump, feeling that he was good for nothing but watching television, he did little else.

Tam was tempted to hug him and tell him not to worry about the mower, that it didn't matter, that she would take care of it.

This was exactly what she could not do. He had to be responsible for doing his own jobs. He needed to work, to have the self-respect that comes from doing a job. It was, however, difficult to get him going now and then.

She said, "You'll have to fix it, Dad. It's embarrassing borrowing Mrs. Warren's mower all the time, getting it dirty when I use it. Promise me you'll fix ours today."

"No."

He neither nodded nor shook his head so she didn't know what he meant. She could push him only so far, though, so she let it go. She didn't have time to argue. She had to do laundry and find something easy for Dad to fix for supper, pack her own supper, get ready for work, and be out the door by two o'clock for the other half of her life.

These halves seemed entirely unconnected, as if she were two separate people living two separate lives. That's what she liked best about her job. It gave her a world away from her worries at home and kept her too busy to think much.

At two, when she left for work, the driveway was empty.

Too bad. She was curious about "the boys" and wanted to get a look at them in the daylight, especially the one with the little sports car—Stewart, the manager. She wondered if he looked like Mack, the manager of Food Mart. Do all managers look alike?

She'd seen enough of the other one, the artist, to know she didn't like him.

Artist. Big deal.

But it was a big deal. That's what hurt her. Bad enough to give up her own dream of studying art without having to live next to a real artist. Painter, Mrs. Warren had said.

Artist, painter—either way he's unemployed. He'll never find a job. Probably doesn't intend to.

She could imagine him applying for a job. "Do you have a job for an artist? Something not too strenuous or time consuming so I don't have to waste my creativity on ordinary triviality?"

He'll never find a job, she thought, *He'll sit up there in that attic and paint and let his friend support him. When Stewart leaves, he'll have Mrs. Warren to mother him. He'll never have to come down to the real world at all.*

Easy life, she thought, *having a friend support you. He must be a nice person, that friend. Not like the painter.*

Tam puzzled over it on the way to work, along with ways to interest Dad into trying harder. On this warm, sunny afternoon people out in their yards nodded or waved as she passed. The walk to work always seemed faster than the walk home. Actually it took longer because, although it was a shortcut, she took her time and enjoyed the walk, even in rain.

Going home in darkness was a different matter. Going home, she hurried.

Work went all right. She was uneasy about the gum incident, but nobody mentioned it and Mack seemed unaware.

Mr. Brill came in and joked around as usual, but he didn't mention stopping for Tam. She was glad. It was bad enough that Barb and Vickie asked her about his teeth as soon as he was out of the store. If they'd known about the ride offer, they'd have teased her all night.

They were always busy on Friday nights. People got paid at the end of the week and seemed to take their money directly to the grocery. Activity made the time go fast; it was eleven before she knew it.

She hurried through dark streets, wishing she had a ride. Once she thought she saw Mr. Brill's car cross the intersection ahead, but she must have been mistaken.

Lights were on in the attic next door when she got home, and both cars were in the driveway. No other lights were on. She stood in the shadows, listening. The street was silent, as it was every night. Except for the attic light and the two cars, nothing was different. Looking from her side door, she saw no silhouette darkening the window.

What was it like to be up there all alone in the still night, painting? With hours to spend and no one to make him feel guilty about spending them on art. Such luxury. *Did he have any idea how lucky he was? Probably not,* she thought.

She sniffed the air for traces of turpentine and linseed oil. but smelled none. Too bad. She liked the smells of painting. Perhaps he used watercolors, which don't have much smell. *If it were me,* she thought, *I'd use oils.*

She thought she might still have some oil paints someplace. It had been a long time since she'd used them.

She and Dad had their tea and went to bed. She turned her pillow to the breeze again and lay staring up at the attic window, wondering. Once she thought she saw his shadow, but maybe not. She promised herself she'd get a good look tomorrow and slept.

She did get a good look the next day, when she went over to borrow Mrs. Warren's lawn mower. She didn't really go over to see "the boys," but she was curious, so when Mrs. Warren asked her in to meet Stewart, she went.

He was tall, tan, blond, lean, and athletic looking, the owner of an intimidating, dazzling smile—a marvel of a man, absolutely everything the driver of that little yellow sports car should be and then some.

He rose from his chair to press Tam's hand and smile into her eyes. He remained standing while she shifted from one foot to the other in embarrassment, wishing for all she was worth that she looked better. If she had known. . .

"Hi," she said in not quite a squeak.

"How do you do, Tam," he said, in smooth rich baritone.

"I. . .uh. . .just came over to borrow the lawn mower again," she stammered. Nobody, she thought, could accuse her of charming him with brilliant conversation.

Mrs. Warren didn't seem to notice Tam's sudden loss of intelligence. She said, "Your dad didn't fix it yet, huh?"

"Not yet," Tam answered, relieved to have something sensible to say. "He will, I think, if I can just get him past this little slump." Tam knew this made no sense to the mass of tan sophistication standing next to her, but it would have to do. "If I could just borrow your mower to do the front yard. . ."

"Sure, Tam. You know where I keep it. Help yourself."

"Let me get it for you," said Tan-With-Teeth.

"No! I mean, no thanks. Thanks anyway." Tam hurried awkwardly out and down the steps, glad to escape.

Stewart was more than she was ready for. She wished she didn't have to cut the grass. Not out in the yard where Stewart could see her and watch her get sweaty. If she had to cut the grass, she wished she could do it inside the house.

She's start on the other side of the house, where Stewart couldn't see her. By the time she finished the hidden part, Stewart might be gone. Then she could sweat all over the front yard without his seeing.

Don't be silly, she told herself. *Everybody sweats.*

Not Stewart, she thought.

He won't look at you, she told herself. *You could push that mower round and round, wearing your best bikini, if you had one, and he wouldn't notice. Grow up. Get out there and cut that grass. Now. Before you lose your nerve.*

She started on the far side. Sure enough the little butter-yellow car hummed out of the driveway just as she finished. With Stewart gone, she zoomed through the front at top speed, anxious to finish and disappear before he came back and caught her sweating in her old cotton skirt and worn blouse.

She didn't need to rush. He wasn't back when she wiped the last blade of grass off the mower and returned it. He wasn't back when she left for work either. Good!

And where was the artist all this time? She wondered. She saw him go out to the van, which in daylight was nondescript blue-black with rust spots. She was cutting back and forth across the front lawn at that time and when she cut back to that side, he and the van were gone.

His attic light was on again when she came home from work that night, and both cars were back. Everything was quiet.

She stopped to gaze up at the light before going in for tea with Dad and wondered it the artist up there was aware of neighbors with concerns that kept them as busy as his painting kept him. She wondered if he cared.

That was Saturday. Sunday was like any other day, a work day. She could do as she pleased in the morning though, if she stayed where Dad could find her.

She thought about going to church. Occasionally she went. Church was only two blocks down the street and one block over, not too far to walk. Dad could do it if they walked slowly. He seemed to enjoy going, but getting him up and ready was not easy.

If he decided he wanted to go to church, he was up and dressed and sitting in the kitchen, tapping his foot for her to hurry. But if he decided he wasn't going, every sock, every button, every little move was fight and not worth the struggle.

That Sunday morning was a struggle, so she quickly gave up. She slid into another old skirt and went to enjoy a leisurely breakfast with the Sunday paper. Pages were already spread out all over the kitchen by her father, who always picked it up from the driveway and read it before Tam woke.

It was raining lightly, and the gravel in the driveway was the dark gray it turned when it got wet, instead of its usual chalky near-white. Mrs. Warren would be getting ready to go teach her primary class and, sipping tea, Tam absently watched for her.

At nine, on the button, Mrs. Warren stepped off the back porch, Sunday school materials and Bible tucked under her arm. With her, resplendent in navy blue blazer and gray flannel trousers, like a fashion ad in the Sunday paper, was Stewart.

He hesitated by the little yellow car. Mrs. Warren shook her head and walked on toward church with her umbrella still furled and swinging by her side.

Tam chuckled. Mrs. Warren was treating her boys exactly as she had her own children. No doubt they would learn to love her too.

What's-his-name-the-artist didn't appear. Tam wondered how he managed to stay home but was willing to guarantee his exemption from church attendance wouldn't last long. Anyone living in the Warren house went to church. It was that simple. When her children used to complain, she always said, "Other people's children may do as they like, '. . .but as for me and my house, we will serve the Lord.'"

It's hard to argue against a mother who quotes Scripture and lives by it, so soon they gave up and began to finish the verse before she did. Later, when they were teenagers, they would say, "We know. . .Joshua 24:15," and would go ahead and get ready for church.

Wait until what's-his-name-the-artist runs up against that, thought Tam.

When Stewart and Mrs. Warren strolled home in the pale sunlight between drizzles, Tam was still in the kitchen with tea and Sunday papers. She spent most of the morning there.

On Sundays Tam cooked with more regard for Dad's taste preferences than during the week, when he adhered strictly to his diet. Sunday was treat time.

She and Dad had their usual weekend tournament of games, mostly Parcheesi this weekend, because he was feeling less confident than he had last week when he had trounced her soundly at checkers. "Children's games" had been part of his therapy long ago and had become one of their rituals. He wanted to play more often, but there was less time for games during the week than there was on weekends.

His heart wasn't really in the games that Sunday, nor in taking a walk or in sitting on the porch. She tried reading to him about whales. He had liked it at the library, but now it didn't appeal to him.

When Tam left for work, Dad was staring at a National Geographic special on gorillas. When Tam returned, they had tea and went to bed. . .a typical Sunday.

The attic was lit when Tam went to bed, again.

She thought she might stay up some night and see what time he turned the light off, *if* he ever did. Maybe he just left it on all the time and wasn't there at all.

Or maybe he never left the attic. Never. Stayed there, day and night, morning and evening, painting, painting.

No wonder he was a grouch. He never slept.

Maybe. Or maybe sleep was all he did. Maybe the story about being an artist was a cover for his abnormal desire to sleep all the time. After all, Tam had only Mrs. Warren's word that he was an artist, and *she* had only Mr. Moore's word, and Mr. Moore had been their pastor for such a short time, a few years. . .

**Okay, so he was an artist.
What did he do up there?**

three

Monday morning's steady gray drizzle lacquered leaves and roofs, bringing out dark tones which sunshine usually glared into hiding. It also lacquered the beat-up van but failed to enhance its miserable looks. *The little yellow car looks sunny in any weather,* thought Tam; but by breakfast time, the little car was gone. The attic light was still on.

Dad's dreary mood persisted. Although he'd rehearsed it for days, he refused to announce "Breakfast is ready," either when breakfast really was ready or later, at his lesson time, but Tam gave him no peace without it.

Slogging through the exercises frustrated both of them. They quit early, with considerable relief.

Few birds appeared, so television began early. Tam forced herself to make the best of a dull day by doing dull jobs. While she worked, she tried to think of a fresh idea to spark Dad's interest. She was still thinking as she left for work in the drizzle.

Tam liked walking in the rain, if the rain was a light rain and the air was warm on her face. Drizzly days sound different, softer, more private. They changed the face of the familiar to something a little mystical, but friendly and cozy.

Walking silently in her hooded slicker, she stopped thinking and let the softness of the rain soothe her. By the time she got to work, she was ready to meet the world again.

38

All evening the few people who came in complained about the weather. About eight it rained harder and the customers were scarce even for a Monday.

With no customers watching, Barb offered Tam some pretzels from a bag she had "borrowed" from the hang-ups near the soft drinks.

"My treat," Tam said.

Barb said, "Don't be stupid. Nobody pays. Pretzels come with the job."

"I can't do that," Tam said, "I feel like a thief."

Barb was insulted. "Is that what you think of me?" Barb demanded. "You're calling me a thief."

"I. . ."

"Listen, Tam; everybody takes. Ask Vickie why she never has to buy toothpaste. Ask Al who opens sweet pickles, eats one and puts the lid back on so on one can tell. Ask anybody."

Tam said. "If it's okay to take them, why not walk out with them in your hand, instead of hiding them from Mack?"

"Mack!" Barb sneered. "He's a manager. Managers aren't regular people like you and me. Managers just care about getting their money's worth out of us. They don't care what we do as long as they make money. What's the matter with you, anyway? I thought we were friends."

Tam said, "We are friends. That's why I don't want you getting in trouble over a couple of packs of gum. You could get fired for that."

Barb laughed. "It won't happen. Trust me. Old Barbara won't get caught, unless you decide to tell on me." She narrowed her eyes in sudden suspicion. "You gonna tell Mack?"

"No," Tam said firmly. "You know I won't."

"Then what's the matter with you, Tam? You been talking to that crazy Hope? You getting religious on us?"

She hit too close to truth and Tam winced, saying, innocently, "What do you mean?"

Back on her favorite subject, Barb sneered, "You know. All that stuff about sin and wickedness—all that Bible stuff. Next thing I know *you'll* be a Christian."

"I am a Christian," Tam said. "Aren't you?"

"You mean like not Jewish or Arab or something? Yeah, I guess I'm Christian. I just don't let it get in my way. What difference does it make, anyway, unless you're getting married or buried or something like that? Even then marriages don't last, no matter how fancy the ceremony is." Tam's dismayed look stopped Barb.

More quietly, to excuse her outburst, Barb said, "If you want to call yourself Christian, Tam, go ahead. Just don't get crazy with it, like Hope does. I think she actually believes that stuff."

"She does," Tam said. "Lots of people do. I go to church myself, sometimes."

"Well, that's different," declared Barb. "You have enough sense not to act like it. Nobody would ever mistake you for a Christian."

"That's funny," Tam said, thinking it was not funny at all. "I always assumed they would."

"Oh, Tam, you say the silliest things."

"That's the artist in me," Tam said, trying to brush off the subject. "I'm serious about the pretzels, though. I worry about you. I'd feel a lot better if you wouldn't do it anymore."

Barb patted Tam on the head, mother to child, "Okay,

honey, I won't do it again. And when I do, I won't tell you about it. How's that?"

Pulling out from under the patting hand, Tam said, "I'd rather you just never did it again. Period."

"Sure, honey, whatever you say. You can even pay for these if it will make you feel better. Now have some."

Tam took some pretzels and went to the office to get change from her purse to pay. Talking with Barb had been every bit as difficult and useless as she'd thought it would be. From now on, Barb would just not tell her.

Okay, thought Tam, *at least I tried.*

Hope came by a couple of times while Tam was on checkout. Tam understood Hope wanted to talk, but Tam didn't—not to Hope. So Tam ignored her and soon Hope went away.

Tam's mind stuck on what Barb had said about Hope's being serious about her Christianity. Hope really believed and that made her different. Barbara wouldn't understand why Hope wanted to be different and what Barbara didn't understand, she didn't like. She didn't like Hope.

Tam realized with a jolt that Barb wouldn't like her either if she were like Hope.

No problem there. No one would ever suspect Tam of being Christian. Barb said so. No one would suspect Tam of actually believing the Bible.

Tam tried to erase that thought but it remained, like a thorn, pricking and itching. She thought everyone knew she was Christian. She'd gone to Sunday school when she was a child. She still went to church now and then. Her mother and father had always gone to church too. Even her neighbors went. What else would she be, if not a Christian?

Having argued the question to this point, she tried again to erase it, but it wouldn't go. As soon as she concluded that of course she must be automatically Christian, the thorn pricked again and she was back to Barbara's statement that no one would suspect it.

So be it, she thought. *My friends like me the way I am; I'm not so bad. I'm religious enough for practical purposes. I don't have time or energy for more than that. Somebody else will have to teach Sunday school and sew for the missionaries. I've got my hands full right here at the checkout counter.*

Tam rang up prices and still the thorn stuck, along with another thought: If it didn't matter, why did it bother her?

She counted out change and pushed the bag over to the customer, then stepped on the conveyor belt pedal to move the next customer's groceries up.

A box of soap and a can of beans. Into the bag.

"Aren't you going to ask if I've forgotten anything?" asked a familiar voice.

Tam looked up to see Mr. Brill smiling at her. "Sure," she said. "Did you forget anything?"

"If I did, I'll get it next time," he said. "Why so serious?"

"Just the rain, I guess," she said, passing it off lightly. "It's coming down hard now. Drive carefully. The roads might be slippery."

"I'll be careful. See you." He took his little bag and nodded. At the electric eye he called a good night and pulled up his collar against the rain before hurrying into the night.

At least Mr. Brill is unchanging, Tam thought. *Dad has moods and Barbara gets mad and I spend too much time worrying about what other people think, but good old Mr.*

Brill never changes.

She yawned and stretched and went to look for something to do. Vickie could manage the front alone. The dairy case stank from leaky milk cartons, so Tam went to clean it. Since no one would come around to talk until they were sure they wouldn't get stuck helping, the unpopular job suited Tam fine. It provided time to think without having to make small talk.

By eleven the milk was neatly arranged in a sparkling clean case. Tam was tired but satisfied with the way it looked. *Mrs. Warren must feel this way when she finishes one of her cleaning jobs,* Tam thought. Mrs. Warren would love to clean the milk case, where she could really see a difference.

Barb and Vickie and Tam punched out together. Tam hadn't talked to Barb since their meeting over the pretzels, and she wanted to make sure they were on friendly terms. If Barb and Vickie were going to stay for a cup of coffee before braving the rain, she'd stay and chat for a bit to kind of ease any leftover bad feeling.

"What's happening?" Tam asked, to open communications. Barb looked at her with a sly smile. "You sure you want to know? You'll be happier if I don't tell you."

"You're right," Tam said. "Don't tell me." She put on her slicker and pulled up the hood. Hope, watching from her corner, said nothing and looked away quickly.

"See you tomorrow," Tam said to no one in particular. She pushed through the swinging door and stamped past the frozens to the front door.

What is the matter with me, she wondered. *I'm stamping around like a two-year-old. Why snap at Barb over an answer no different from dozens of other answers I've gotten from her?*

She felt awkward and foolish and wondered if she should go back and apologize.

What a day! First Dad and his moods, then a fight with Barbara, and now Tam had made a fool of herself. *I should go back and straighten things out before I leave,* she thought.

As she started back through the frozens, she heard Vickie say, "What's wrong with Tam?"

Barb's voice was closer. "Oh, nothing. She 's probably just worried about her Dad. You know how she. . ."

At the end of the aisle the three girls met and for an awkward moment stared at each other. Barb spoke, "Walking out with us, Tam?"

The three walked to the front together, as usual, and stopped at the door. "See ya," they all said. Taking huge breaths in unison, they plunged into the cold, heavy curtain of rain, half-running their separate directions.

To see where she was going, Tam had to look up. To keep dry, she had to keep her head down. She compromised by peering out from her hood, and it wasn't bad until the blackness at the end of the lighted lot.

She thought quickly of those extra blocks through town, balancing them against the darkness of the shorter way through neighborhood streets. She feared those dark side streets, but the main streets would be dark in the rain too. It was about even.

She went left, away from the lighted streets of town, moving faster down the black tunnel under the trees.

It was inky black, scary. With no one out, not even the neighborhood dogs, the night was deserted, silent except for her breathing and the hollow echo of her footsteps. The only signs of human existence were eerie green-blue glows from television screens and an occasional yellowish light from a lamp.

If anyone is out here, hiding, waiting. . .

Don't be silly, she told herself. *No one with any sense would be out here in this wet.*

She began to jog.

Behind her, car tires sizzled on the street and came to a stop next to her at the curb. She kept on running, catching a quick look over shoulder, hoping a local resident was coming home, parking in front of his, her, own house.

The car did not stop. It crept along next to her, keeping up with her. She ran faster.

"Tam? Tam! It's me, Mr. Brill. Get in and I'll take you home."

"Mr. Brill? Is that really you?" She stood there, dripping, uncertain.

"It's really me. Get in." He reached across and opened the door.

She saw the light on his face and recognized him. She got in.

"You're all wet," he said, setting the car in motion before she shut the door. "Put your seat belt on. Now that I've got you in here, I don't want to take a chance on losing you." He laughed a little as she pulled hard against the door to shut it and began to fumble with the unfamiliar seat belt.

"Pull the buckle over to the middle and snap it in that slot," he instructed.

The belt wouldn't pull longer. She tugged again and again and each time she heard it click solidly to a stop. He reached across her and drew the buckle slowly to the middle and locked it firmly into the slot. "There," he said. "You just have to know how it works."

He drove slowly, his headlights making a path through blackness that enveloped them in the capsule of his car. Dim illumination from the dash lit his face from below, giving him a ghostly appearance.

He snapped the radio on and romantic music filled the capsule. He smiled and she smiled back, tightly, not quite comfortable. Nothing was wrong exactly, nothing specific, but. . .

He turned left at the next corner, and right at the next one, the way she usually walked home.

"How did you know where to turn?" she asked.

He smiled smugly. "I know the way you walk to work and the way you walk home. I know where you live. I've known for some time now."

Tam shivered. "You've been watching me."

"Are you cold?" he asked. "Let me turn on some heat."

He fiddled with some knobs and hot dry air blasted her ankles. She winced. He turned the heat down.

She slid her left hand slowly down to feel for the seat belt slot. "How long?" she asked. Her fingers followed the belt to its release button. She held the belt away from her with her right hand and pressed the button, shuffling her feet to cover its noise. The belt jumped and she stiffened so she didn't jump too. She held it fast and eased her left hand up to grip the edge of the seat. "How long have you been following me?"

"A long time now, Tam. I like to know where my friends go."

"Why didn't you ever tell me?"

"You weren't ready," he said. "I couldn't tell you till you

were ready."

She shivered harder, her teeth starting to chatter. "I'm still not ready. I don't like this."

He reached over to stroke her hand where it curled in a fist on the edge of the seat. "Don't be afraid," he said, in a chillingly caressing tone. "I'm your friend. You know I won't hurt you." He stroked her hand as he talked.

For a moment she froze, her breath sticking in her throat. Then she pulled her hand away from his and gathered her purse from her lap. "Let me out. I'll walk the rest of the way."

He kept driving. "I can't let you do that."

"Yes, you can," she pleaded. "I'm only a few blocks from home now."

"No," he said, shaking his head quickly. "No. Why don't you want to ride with me? I thought you were my friend."

"I am. I just want to walk." The seat belt zipped away as she let go to pull at the door handle. "I want to get out of here."

"No!" He stepped on the accelerator and the car leaped forward, throwing her back against the seat.

She had to get out.

At the corner he slammed on the brakes for the stop sign and she would have been thrown against the dash, but she was ready this time. When he squealed to a stop, she flung open the door and jumped out, landing on her hands and knees in the wet street. She scrambled to her feet and began to run.

Behind her a car door opened and she heard him shout, "Stop! Come back!"

She didn't stop, didn't look back. She ran through the deep puddle by the curb and up onto the grass, where he could not drive to follow. She dodged into some tall bushes between two houses and stopped, still, listening for his step.

Nothing.

Cautiously, she pulled aside the branch in front of her face and looked for him, expecting him to be looking back at her from the other side of the bushes. She saw nothing on the lawn.

The car sat at the corner. She couldn't see it, but she could tell where it was by the illumination from the headlights and the faint sound of the radio. She stood absolutely still, not breathing more than she absolutely had to. Listening. Watching.

All was quiet but the rain and the sounds of the car.

Slam! A pause and then Slam! again as the two car doors shut. The engine raced and tires squealed as Mr. Brill tore off.

Tam's chest hurt from holding her breath and her heart pounded loudly in her ears. She gasped, drawing in great ragged breaths, then scraped through the bushes to the open lawn.

Without the car lights, the street was totally dark and for the first time she was grateful for the cover of the night. If Mr. Brill came back, he would have a hard time seeing her.

A dog barked inside the nearest house, the bark bringing sharper awareness of her isolation. If she hadn't just escaped from a "friend," she might have asked for help. She considered it, but she didn't know these people.

They might let her use the phone, but she had no one to call. Dad couldn't come get her; he no longer dared drive and had no car. The police? Mr. Brill was gone and she was unhurt. The police would think she was imagining things, afraid of shadows. A taxi? Only four blocks from home?

She might as well walk. Or run.

Experimentally moving her legs, she discovered that she had difficulty moving them in smooth coordination. She was shaking, wobbly. Her knees hurt. She peered at them in the dark, but couldn't see them. She must have scraped them when she fell, scraped her hands, too, judging by the way they stung.

Wobbly or not, she had to get home before Mr. Brill came back looking for her. He knew where she lived. He might be along the way, waiting, even in front of her house. There was no way to know what he would do.

Before tonight, Tam would never have believed that this little man with thin gray hair and the beginnings of a pot belly would be dangerous. Fifteen minutes in his car had changed her mind.

She tested her legs again, bending her knees a little more than necessary for walking. They seemed all right. She sloshed across the lawn, water squishing loudly in her shoes.

The sidewalk was easier going, but her regular determined stride was too much for her damaged, unreliable knees. She wobbled along, heedless of puddles and careful of curbs and rough places, keeping to the darker side of the street. The last block, her own, she greeted with a smothered cry of relief and broke into a hobbling kind of run.

Mr. Brill was nowhere to be seen. Reaching Mrs. Warren's driveway she whooped aloud with joy at being home and safe. The crunch of gravel beneath her feet was the sound of home.

Then she fell, tripping over some invisible bump and landing smash on the driveway, parked like a very small third car behind that dismal-looking van.

Somewhere a door opened and a screen door slammed, but she didn't care. She was home and in a minute she would get up and go in and have tea, just as she always did. Everything would be all right.

She propped herself up on one hand and pulled her legs under herself to get up. Footsteps crunched gravel to her right. She jerked around to see blue jeans approaching. She looked up past jeans and T-shirt to an unfamiliar face. She held up her free arm to protect herself and tried to crawl across the gravel toward her own door. "No, she whispered hoarsely. "No."

"Be still! It's only me. . .Luke."

"Luke?"

"Your neighbor. I moved into Mrs. Warren's house last week," he said. "Come on. Let's get you inside."

Huge, warm hands under her arms lifted her as if she were weightless and stood her on her feet, where she swayed dizzily. A familiar pungent odor tickled her nose. Turpentine. "Luke?" she puzzled aloud. "What's-his-name-the-painter?"

"That's me: What's-his-name-the-painter. Easy does it. I'd better carry you. Hold on."

With that he picked her up and held her against his chest, bumping along with her face against the T-shirt, to a door. He pulled at the knob with the hand nearest it and caught the door open with his foot. Then they were inside Mrs. Warren's kitchen.

He set her on the kitchen counter like a small child and backed away to get a good look at her. "You're a mess," he said. "You're soaking wet."

She blinked in the bright fluorescent light, looking away quickly from those too perceptive brown eyes.

"Are you hurt?"

She shook her head, looking at the floor.

"Let me see those hands," he said, taking one of her fists and opening it in the light. "You've scraped this one. Let's see the other. This one's worse. Sit right here while I get something to clean that up with." He reached to the sink to put some warm water and soap on a paper towel.

While he was turned partly away from her, not looking through her with those eyes of his, she took a long, direct look.

He was huge. Perhaps it was only because at that moment she felt so small and helpless, but she thought she had never anyone that big before. She was positive she had never been this close to anyone that big.

He was tall, 6'2" or more, and his T-shirt-covered shoulders were massive. They tapered to a trim, unbelted waist in a smooth line unbroken by bulges or ripples of flab. He looked like the result of hundreds of hours lifting weights. No wonder he had carried her so easily. Her 115 pounds must have felt like nothing in his arms.

In his arms, she thought, and her stomach felt the way it did in a fast elevator descent—as if the bottom had dropped out of it.

As he turned back to her, she looked away. The nearness of this huge man in Mrs. Warren's kitchen confused her. She was embarrassed, sitting there making puddles on the countertop and floor with the run-off her dripping clothes, and she was confused. She was not frightened.

How odd, she thought, *to feel safe with this huge stranger after being frightened by little Mr. Brill.*

She held out her hand for the towel to clean the scrapes, but Luke took her hand in his great paw and gently dabbed at the raw flesh with the towel.

She sat perfectly still while he did first one hand and then the other. The memory of Mr. Brill's touch on her hand made her stomach turn over. She shuddered.

Luke stopped immediately and looked sharply at her. "Hurt?"

She shook her head.

"You're shaking," he said. "You're cold sitting there in those wet things. We'll get you home as soon as we can." He paused. "You must have fallen harder than I thought."

He looked at her again, more closely. "That's not it, is it." His statement required no answer. She gave none. "What's happened to you?" he asked.

She tried to avoid his steady, searching look by twisting away, but he took her trembling chin in his warm hand and turned her face up so she had to meet his gaze directly.

"What happened?" he repeated.

Her face grew hot in his hand and she knew she was blushing. That knowledge made her blush more. She shut her eyes against his closeness, but the tangy smell of turpentine and oil paint, and the firm hand on her chin, made it impossible to shut him out. She tried to shake her head but it was too firmly held. When she opened her eyes, he was still watching for an explanation.

"What happened?" he persisted. His voice was not as gruff as she remembered it from the night he shouted at her from the attic window, but it was every bit as deep and commanding. This was a man accustomed to giving orders.

She jerked her head up and free and pulled away. "I was hurrying and I tripped," she answered.

"Yes? And more than once, I think," he said. "Your hands and knees have black marks on them, like you've scraped them on blacktop. The gravel isn't black."

"My knees. Oh." Tam had forgotten them, but now she saw that they, too, were scraped and bleeding. "I jumped out of the car."

"Now we come to the real problem," he said, beginning to dab carefully at her blackened knees. She reached again for the paper towel and pulled away from his touch, but he brushed away her hands and continued dabbing. "Go on. Let's hear it."

So she told him the whole miserable thing—about nice little Mr. Brill who wasn't nice after all, and about jumping out at the stop sign, and about the bushes and running home and all of it—nonstop, talking without interruption while he cleaned her scrapes and treated them with something from Mrs. Warren's perfectly ordered first aid kit.

When her story was finished, she was trembling and close to tears. Tam was long past the stage where she cried easily, but she felt the tears in the back of her tight throat, could hear them in her voice. They didn't come to her eyes.

"Didn't anyone ever tell you not to accept rides from strangers?" Luke scolded angrily.

Tam's anger rose in defense. "He wasn't a stranger. I thought he was a friend. I saw him many times and he was always nice. I've seen you only once. I know him better than I know you. How do I know what you're really like? For all I know you're as bad as he is. Worse, maybe."

He studied her in silence and she glared back at him, taking in his shaggy chestnut hair and straight brows and paint-splotched shirt. It was difficult to focus directly on those wise brown eyes.

When she did, she saw his anger give way to a flicker of amusement. She thought it was amusement. His expression hadn't really altered, but he seemed less stern somehow. When he spoke the gruffness was there, but not as fierce as his scolding had been.

"You're right. You don't know me," he said. "And I don't know you. You might be making all this up just to get in here to rob Mrs. Warren."

"I wouldn't do that. That's ridiculous," she scoffed.

He shrugged those giant shoulders. "How do I know?"

"Ask Mrs. Warren," she said.

"Good idea," he said, moving toward the stairs. "I'll wake her up and ask her."

"No, don't wake her up. You can ask her in the morning. I'll just go home and leave you alone and you won't have to worry about being robbed." Tam wriggled toward the edge of the counter to hop down.

He caught her mid-hop and eased her to her feet. "Independent, aren't you?" he said.

"I have to be," she answered. "And I have to get home. Dad will be worried about me."

He nodded. "He should be. What you need is dry clothes and some hot coffee. Can you walk, or should I carry you?"

"I'll walk," she said, remembering the strength of those arms and the feel of his shirt against her cheek.

"Of course," he said, sounding amused.

Tam looked at the puddles she had made. What a mess. She reached for the roll of paper towels to mop it up. He put them out of her reach on the counter. "Later," he said.

"Let's get you home."

It was still pouring outside. She said, "I'll go; you stay here. No point in both of us getting wet."

"Too late. I'm already wet," he pointed out.

He was, especially where he had held her against his shirt. Looking more closely, she realized that some of the paint on his shirt was blood. Hers. Not thinking about what she was doing, she reached out to brush at the spot on his sleeve. His arm was warm beneath her touch. She stopped.

She could feel the blush begin and ducked to hide it, pulling back from him. He caught her hand as she pulled away and held it for a long second. Neither spoke. Then he released her hand. He pushed her toward the door and opened it, ushering her out into the rain with one arm loosely around her shoulders.

Across the gravel they went, Tam hopping while Luke held her more or less off the ground so her hops were moonwalk long. At her door he let her go and waited for her to open it with the key she kept in her purse.

Purse. She didn't have her purse. She felt for it frantically, but there was no place for it to be.

"My purse," she said. "I must have dropped it."

Luke was out in the driveway and back with the dripping purse before she had moved more than two feet from the door.

"Good thing it's plastic," he said, handing it to her.

She groped around in the soggy bag for the key. "Here it is," she said, and opened the door to the dimly lit kitchen.

"I don't keep coffee in the house," she said, "but I have tea. Would you like a cup of tea?"

"No, thanks. What I want is for you to get out of those

wet things as soon as possible, before you get pneumonia and blame it on me."

"I. . . Thanks," she began. "Thanks for. . ."

"Nothing," he finished. "I couldn't leave you lying in the driveway, could I? I'm just glad I heard you cry out."

She mumbled, "I'm so embarrassed."

He looked at her and through her with those serious eyes, and said softly, "Don't ever be embarrassed with me. Or afraid. Ever." He touched her bedraggled hair tentatively with two fingertips. "Get into dry clothes. Now." And he was gone.

For a moment she stood in the silence of the empty kitchen, half expecting him to materialize out of the dark again, but he didn't. She touched her hair where he had touched it, and felt it wet and stringy against her raw palm.

She sighed. Relief, of course, she told herself. Why else would she sigh?

Suddenly conscious of the cold wetness of her clothes against her shivering goose-flesh, she moved to follow Luke's orders, to get out of those wet clothes and into something dry.

Dad wasn't worried about her at all. In dry robe and slippers, she sat with him in the quiet kitchen and he filled her in on the day's quiz shows. She didn't tell Dad about Luke-the-painter or Mr. Brill. He didn't ask about her scrapes. He seemed to notice neither them nor the fact that she said almost nothing.

four

In the morning, nothing was left of Tam's adventures but raw hands and knees and some sore muscles. Both car and van were gone. The attic light was out. The rain had stopped and, except for puddles and general wetness, there was no trace of yesterday on the face of her world. It might never have happened.

Twenty-seven-years-old and already senile, she thought. *You really have some imagination. You probably thought poor old Mr. Brill had wicked plans for you. You must have scared him as badly as he scared you.* She pictured him standing in the rain next to his car, calling for her, wondering where she'd gone, finally giving up and going home. She supposed he went home, unless he had followed another girl and offered rides to her.

She laughed aloud over her toast, startling both herself and Dad. She looked up to find him watching her, puzzled. She laughed again, this time at herself. She was middle-aged and definitely showing it, dirty and tired from work last night, smelling of the milk case and dripping wet. And she imagined herself attractive to that little man. She must have looked a sight.

She laughed again. This time Dad laughed cautiously with her, keeping a wary eye on this peculiar daughter who laughed over toast.

He picked up the other piece of her toast and inspected it, both sides, and put it back. Nothing funny about the toast. He waited.

I really have to stop being so silly, she thought. *This isn't senility. It's delayed adolescence. Only a teenager would leap from a car at a stop sign. Or lurk about in bushes. Or fall down and scrape hands and knees. An eight-year-old might, but an eight-year-old wouldn't just lie there in the driveway looking like a refugee from a war-torn country. An eight-year-old or a teenager would have enough sense to get up and go into the house before a neighbor had to come out and get her.*

What do I mean, "had to"? she thought. *Nobody asked him to come out there in the wet and pick me up... and hold me... next to his chest. . . . and carry me in.*

His arms were strong, she remembered. *He hardly felt her weight. He was gruff, not smiling, but he wasn't as terrible as I expected. He was. . .nice.*

I must have looked awful, she thought.

It was dark. Maybe he didn't see her.

Of course he did. It was plenty bright in Mrs. Warren's kitchen. When he first saw her, he said, "You're a mess."

Oh, she thought, *I wish it hadn't been Luke-the painter who found me.* In the same second she was glad it was Luke instead of Stewart, smooth, blond, handsome Stewart. She'd have died of humiliation if it had been Stewart.

Too bad it wasn't Mrs. Warren. She was used to mishaps and would have known exactly what to do. It wouldn't have upset Mrs. Warren at all. Actually Luke hadn't seemed upset either, except for being a little angry. He behaved as if rescuing people were natural. He was kind, too. Even Mrs. Warren couldn't have been kinder.

Still, she wished he hadn't seen her bedraggled and battered. She blushed. She could never look him in the face again. She hadn't been able to look him in the face last night, either.

That little speech she had made about having to be independent didn't help, especially when she followed it by telling him she'd lost her purse. So much for independence. At least she'd had the presence of mind to thank him, although he'd brushed it off as nothing. She thought of him standing there, telling her not to be embarrassed, not ever, with him. She sighed.

He was nice to me, she thought. *Oh well, he probably would have done the same for a dog. He probably thought I was a dog.*

She hoped, she really hoped, she wouldn't see him again. Ever.

She almost got her wish.

Dad wasn't doing much talking that day and Tam didn't want to talk either. They meandered through the lesson, both preoccupied with private thoughts. Dad wasn't putting much effort into the lessons and she had no idea how to pull him back to caring.

She was dragging him along, doing all the work while he resisted. They were both glad when the lesson was finished and he could go out on the back porch to check the bird population.

Mrs. Warren didn't come over, so Tam supposed Luke hadn't told her Tam was the one who had messed up her kitchen. Either that or she was too busy cleaning up the mess and restoring the glow to the kitchen floor to discuss the condition of Tam's knees.

When Tam went over to borrow the car for the regular visit to the clinic and the library, Mrs. Warren was indeed busy with the kitchen floor. She didn't mention the puddle, though, or Tam's scrapes.

The next day Tam had to go back to work. The day off helped her get some distance from her scare, but even in daylight, Tam dreaded the walk to work. Dread it or not, she had to go, and the short way was the best way for her knees. She left a little early so she could walk slowly.

Would Mr. Brill come in? She wondered if he would have the nerve. Or did he think she was the one who should apologize? He might think that she had insulted him.

I'm never going to get in that car of his again, she thought. *Never. Even if he follows me home every step of the way.* She shuddered. *He might, but not through that neighborhood. She wouldn't go that way in the dark any more, even in a hail storm. He mightn't be so bold on brighter streets. Of course, he had stopped her on the main street once before. Perhaps the lights wouldn't help at all.*

Later, she thought. *I'll worry about it later. One thing at a time. First I go to work and do my job, then I worry about getting home.*

Punching keys on the register wasn't bad, but bagging and lifting the groceries hurt her hands. She was glad it was a slow night and she could spend most of it stamping prices on cans. Of course Barb and Vickie had to know what had happened to her hands and then so did everybody else. Tam told them. She thought it best they know about Mr. Brill in case he ever tried anything again. She thought Barb would joke about it, but she didn't, and so neither did Vickie. Tam didn't tell about the driveway part, though, or about Luke. She wanted to keep that event to herself a while and savor it. She hadn't told anybody.

Mr. Brill didn't show up and it was just as well. Barb was in a crazy mood and when she got in that mood, she would do anything. She might threaten to beat him up or call the police or even dare him to try anything funny with her.

By break time Barb was winding up to something, anything, casting about for mischief to get into. She found it when Al put money into the coffee machine and pushed selection buttons to get himself a cup of coffee. Out came the coffee, straight out—a horizontal shower of hot coffee that sprayed most of the front of his smock. His smock was always messy, so it was no big loss. Nobody was hurt. After the initial shook, it was funny.

Al looked so surprised standing there with the empty cup in his hand and a whole smockful of coffee all over him. He laughed too. What else was there to do?

He took a lot of kidding about whether or not he got the cream and sugar and about wringing the coffee out of his smock. Comments like that, all in fun. By the time he went back to the produce, Barb and Vickie and Tam ached from laughing.

That's when Hope came in. She almost asked what was funny, but she caught herself. She should have been even more cautions. Barb's unusually friendly tone should have warned her.

Barb said, sweetly, "Hello, Hope. How's the meat section doing tonight?"

Vickie and Tam exchanged glances. Barb was up to something. Hope didn't suspect a thing.

"Not too busy," said Hope. "How's the front?" She looked mystified by this sudden friendliness, but her pleasure was evident.

"Can't complain," said Barb, still sweet. "How about some coffee?"

Hope obviously couldn't believe her luck. In all the time

she'd worked there, neither Barb nor Vickie had shown any interest in her except as an object of insult and scorn. Now they seemed friendly. She smiled, warming to Barb's sweet tone and kind words. "Thanks. I'd like some coffee," she answered. "How about you? I'm buying."

"Sure," said Barb. "I take just sugar."

Hope dug in her pocket for change and came up with some coins, which she began inserting in the slots. Barb watched, grinning. Tam looked at Vickie, who began to grin too. Hope's hand was on the red rectangular button.

"No," Tam began, reaching out to stop Hope. "Don't. . ."

"Hmmm?" said Hope, turning around, her hand still on the button that would trigger the fountain of hot coffee.

"Don't. . .Ow!" Barb's foot crunched down on Tam's, cutting off Tam's warning.

"Oh," said Hope, pushing the button, and then "OH!" as the hot coffee hit her, catching her higher than it had caught Al, because she was smaller. Coffee spat all over her smock, her neck, her arm, the side of her face, and her hair. It hurt. Tam saw the pain in her face and jumped to help, grabbing for the rag they had used to mop up Al's coffee bath.

Barb beat Tam to it, patting and mopping with the rag, slathering Hope with unctuous sympathy. "Oh, Hope," Barb gushed, "What happened? Oh, how awful. Let me help you. Oh, how did this happen?"

Vickie was a step behind, but only a step. She didn't have the rag, but she had honeyed words to pour on Hope's discomfort.

Tam was sickened by the cruelty of Barb's act and the charade of kindness. Hope was helpless in their hands. Tam's stomach twisted and she reacted with sudden anger.

Grasping Hope's arm, she jerked her out of their reach, shoving Hope into the tiny bathroom and locking the door. Tam leaned on the door, staring at Hope, who stared back, confused and hurt.

"What. . ."

With a shake of her head Tam turned Hope to the sink. Hot water for coffee stains? Cold water? Tam couldn't remember. But cold water for burns. It made no difference; the water from both faucets was room temperature.

"Here, give me your smock." Tam said. "You can wear my clean one. I'll wash this one and bring it back. Some of those splashes burned your cheek, I think, and your neck too. I'll get the first aid kit from the office." Tam caught Hope's eye in the mirror. "Sorry I was so rough with you."

"It's all right, Tam. Thanks."

"Don't thank me. This wouldn't have happened if I'd stopped you instead of just standing there. I. . ." She shrugged in apology.

Hope smiled gently. "Thanks."

Hurrying for the first aid kit, Tam pushed through the sympathy squad, Barbara and Vickie. Their kindness had given way to hilarity and they leaned against the wall laughing, repeating fragments of the incident to each other.

"Hey," gloated Barb, catching Tam's arm. "What do you think? Wasn't that the funniest thing you ever saw? Did you see her face when the coffee hit her?"

Vickie added, "The best part was the way we gave her all that help and she just stood there looking stupid."

Barbara said, "I loved it when you grabbed her and shoved her into the bathroom without a word. You really did a job on her. Good going, Tam."

Tam shook herself free.

Barb stopped laughing. "Hey, what's the matter?"

Tam wanted to say how ashamed she felt, wanted to shout at them. She couldn't think of anything to say. She walked off.

After that Tam avoided all of them, even Mack and Al, who had nothing to do with it. Eventually she would have to talk to them. First she needed time to think through, to make sense of her feelings before she tried to defend them. There was no question that she would have some defending to do, to herself and to others.

Defending her own actions was the hard part. Impossible. Sure Tam wanted to protect her friendships by going along with a joke. Yes, she tried to tell Hope not to push the button, and no, she didn't realize the coffee would burn her skin. Not enough. Tam could have stopped her if she had risked the anger of her friends.

Since when am I so afraid of losing my friends that I do things I'm ashamed of? Tam wondered. *What's happened to me?*

She had changed. These were her only friends and it was extremely unlikely that her world would provide others. She was trying to make the best of what she had. That's all. She didn't have much, but she wanted to keep it.

Even if she was ashamed? She was—for herself and for Barbara and Vickie, although they seemed to have no sense of having done wrong by causing pain.

That was the heart of the problem. They didn't feel the way Tam did and wouldn't understand her explanation. They would see her as snobby and unfriendly and would never forgive her.

Tam wouldn't tell them how she felt. No one would ever

know she felt different than they felt.

No one would ever suspect, just like no one would ever suspect she was Christian. Barb had said that. It was supposed to be a compliment but it was a thorn, because it was true.

Tam thought of Mrs. Warren and they way she lived, and of Hope. They weren't like Barbara, not like Tam. They were different.

Their lives are easier, Tam thought. *They aren't shut into their own little corners with family to care for and almost no friends to make the caring easier.*

Nonsense, Tam thought. *That's self-pity, not good sense. Mrs. Warren is more alone than I am, or she was until the boys moved in. Her caring has made my life easier for years. It's simply the way Mrs. Warren is. Hope too. Different.*

Perhaps going to church all the time did that, kept you more aware of other people's needs and weaknesses. It probably helped to have the church behind you when things got tough, too.

Sunday maybe I'll go, thought Tam. *Church didn't do much for me before, but if I had a different church. . . I'll ask Hope where she goes and try that church, if it isn't too far to walk.*

Meanwhile, she had Barbara and Vickie to deal with. She couldn't hide behind the corn flakes forever. Barbara was coming down the aisle with a basket of orphans. If Mack asked what she was doing, Barb would say she was returning misplaced items. Tam would have said Barb was looking for her.

"What's wrong with you?" Barb demanded, stopping almost nose to nose with Tam.

Now or never, Tam thought, and plunged in. "I don't like what we did to Hope. I feel mean and ashamed of myself. We shouldn't have done it."

Barb said, "You're talking about me, aren't you? I'm the one you think is mean."

Tam said, "I'm talking about me, and you, and Vickie. All three of us. We shouldn't have done it. It might be all right if you did it to me; I know we're friends and it's okay if we pull tricks on each other. Hope didn't know it was a trick. She really believed you were being nice to her. It wasn't funny. I felt sorry for her."

She paused to let her words sink in and then went on. "She got burned," Tam said. "Did you know that? In red patches on her face and neck."

"Yeah," sneered Barb, "and I bet she whimpered around plenty about it too. Probably filled your ears with stories about how mean I am to her."

"She didn't say a word," Tam said. "We shouldn't have done it."

Barb wasn't going to admit she was wrong without an argument. "Hmph! She's been asking for it for a long time with that sweet little girl act of hers. I finally got her. That's the truth and you know it."

"Why?" Tam asked.

"Why?" echoed Barb. "She's so. . . You know."

Tam persisted. "No, I don't know. What did she ever do to you?"

"It isn't what she did. It's what she is."

"Nice?" Tam suggested.

"Yeah, sticky sweet, nicey nice. Yecchh."

"Happy?"

"Yeah, that too. Always humming those little tunes

under her breath. And smiling. Normal people don't smile that much. All those sparkling teeth make me nervous."

"How about young? And pretty?" Tam said.

"She's not so pretty," Barb said, "And as for being young, she can have it. It wasn't all that great being y.... Wait a a minute. What are you trying to say?"

Tam said, "I'm saying that you don't like her because she's young and pretty and nice and happy and all the other things that we're not and wish we were. That's it, isn't it? You hate her for having all the things you'd give your right arm to have."

"Me!" Barb exploded. "Me! What about you? Don't stand there and tell me how I think. You're no better than I am."

"You're right, Barb," Tam agreed. "I'm not one bit better. I'd change places with Hope right now if I could. I hate being like this. Only it's not her fault that she has everything and we don't. She probably doesn't even know how well off she is. It's no use hating her for what she can't help being."

Barb regarded Tam as if she were a stranger. At last Barb said, "She's poisoned your mind against me. I thought you were my friend."

"I am."

"No, you're not, or you wouldn't take her side against me. I thought you were my friend."

"That's what Mr. Brill said," Tam mumbled.

"Yeah? Well, I know how he feels." Another glare and Barb flounced off down the aisle, ditching her orphans into a bin of pudding mixes.

Tam shook her head, wondering why she hadn't kept her mouth shut. Life was so much easier when she went along with people and didn't try to go her own direction.

Tam had been going along with her mouth shut for so long that it was almost second nature with her. Almost. She didn't know what had happened to make her speak up this time unless it was the craziness with Mr. Brill. Or being lifted from the gravel by Luke.

She sighed. *That must be it,* she thought. *That would unsettle anyone, especially a person whose life is the same day after day, year after year.*

Suddenly her whole life was changing. She didn't know if she liked that. Handsome, blond, sophisticated Stewart next door, and Luke-the-painter, and Barb's temper, and Hope. . . Tam wasn't sure she was ready for that much change. Things were beginning to get too complicated for comfort.

Business picked up around 9:30 and Mack opened up all three registers. For more than an hour they kept busy. Ordinarily they found time to exchange comments and laugh back and forth, but that night they were all business. Even Al, who always had something to say, packed for Tam without a word.

Mack was around, close. Tam saw him out of the corner of her eye now and then as he lingered in the front of the store. *He knows something's wrong,* she thought. Tam had gone to the office for the first aid kit, so he knew somebody had been hurt. Those searching eyes of his ought to have seen the red spots on Hope's face by now, although if he didn't know what to look for, he might not notice them.

Nobody would tip him off.

As he passed close to Barb, Tam caught her glance. Barb's look asked if Tam had told him about the hot coffee incident. Tam shook her head and Barb looked away.

Mack lingered, straightening magazines, rearranging candy bars, keeping ears and eyes open, especially near Barb.

He didn't hear much. He must have been as sharply aware of the absence of play as everyone else was, but that was the only clue anyone gave. He didn't see much either. The checkers worked together as usual, checking prices, sharing bags or pencils.

They were terribly helpful and polite, all four of them in the front—Barb, Vickie, Al, and Tam. Hope was back in the meat section, so they didn't have a chance to see if Mack took a good look at those red spots.

When things eased up a bit, Mack sent Al back to help clean out the meat cases and took Al's place as packer. He packed only when the front was desperate for help and they weren't, so Tam knew he was hanging around for some reason other than packing.

"How are your hands?" Mack asked, trying to sound casual.

Tam held up her palms for him to see.

"Show him your knees, Tam," called Barbara.

"Never mind," said Mack, and left for the office, where he stayed till almost eleven. Then he reappeared next to the time clock. He fiddled with the time cards, watching each punch out, returning their goodnights in a preoccupied manner.

Hope left first, obviously glad to be out of there. Tam was a close second. Tam wanted Barb to know that if there was trouble, Tam didn't cause it, so she made sure not to speak separately with Mack. Tam and Hope walked through the frozens together, talking of meat, the 9:30 rush—unimportant things. Nearing the ice cream, Tam said, very casually, as if she said things like that all the time, "Say, Hope, you go to church, don't you?"

Hope smiled. "I do. It makes my whole week so right."

"You're not doing so well this week," Tam pointed out.

Hope laughed. "I know what you mean. It's not all bad, though, and the week's not over."

Tam said, "You must go to a pretty good church if you like it that much. Where do you go?"

"Same place you go. Didn't you know?" said Hope. "Mr. Moore asked if I knew you when he found out I work here. I haven't seen you there, though. You must sit in the back."

Tam nodded. In the back. Whenever she went she sat where Dad could be near the door. He liked to be first out.

"I'll look for you next Sunday," said Hope. "Maybe we can sit together. I'll sit in the back if you like." She smiled another of her guileless smiles.

Tam seriously considered it. She was curious about what Hope got out of going to church that she hadn't gotten. Maybe this Sunday, Tam thought, as Hope went through the automatic door.

Tam hesitated, nervously rubbing her scraped palms on her skirt and shifting uneasily from one foot to the other. She had put Mr. Brill from her thoughts, pushing to the back corner of her mind her fears of seeing him pull up alongside the curb next to her. Since the coffee "accident" Tam had been so distracted by other problems that she had forgotten until now that she was going to walk home in the night again. Now she was going to have to do exactly that. She was more afraid than she had expected she would be.

"Scared?"

Tam jumped at Barb's gibe.

"Scared big bad Mr. Brill will get you?" jeered Barb.

"Yes," Tam said.

Barb looked at Tam uncertainly. The jeer faded to concern. Barb said, more softly, "I'd be scared too. Be careful."

Tam began, "Barb, I want. . . ."

"Don't tell me about it," Barb said. "I'm not in a mood for any more talk. And don't start thinking we're still friends just because I don't want you to get hurt on the way home. Come on, Vickie."

Vickie was right behind her. "Coming. Nite, Tam." She slid past, looking uncomfortable, then came to a complete halt with the automatic door stuck wide open. "Wow," she said. "It's Prince Charming."

Tam looked in the direction of Vickie's stare to see what it was that had stopped her. So did Barbara, who said, probably loud enough for Prince Charming to hear, "Wow is the right word, all right. Definitely wow. Who is he?"

Tam knew. She recognized the little yellow car from Mrs. Warren's driveway, the blond wavy hair, the perfect good looks of the driver who lounged in careless elegance against the passenger door. Stewart.

Of all people to see me like this, she thought. She took a deep breath and said to herself: *Try to act like a grown-up this time.* She tentatively waggled her hand in feeble greeting through the window. He waved back and in one fluid motion opened the car door. He didn't actually bow, but the effect was the same.

As Tam came cautiously through the door, he asked, "May I offer you a ride home?"

"Yes," said Barbara and Vickie in unison. Tam discovered she had no voice. She nodded.

Tam floated...well, all right, she walked carefully....past Barb, who murmured as Tam passed, "And to think I was worried about how you would get home."

Tam didn't answer. She was concentrating on floating gracefully to the car. It wasn't easy to float without falling over her own feet. She hadn't had much practice recently.

"T.T.I." Her high school gym teacher's old admonition to "Tuck Tummy In" popped into her head from nowhere, along with her mother's lesson that a lady always walks with her back straight, and somebody-or-other's instruction to keep her head up. Tam tried to do everything at once and still look calm. Floating.

Walking is a difficult exercise, once the walker begins thinking about how to do it. Tam frowned with the effort and found herself standing, at last, next to the car, frowning down at the pavement.

"May I offer you a ride home?" he repeated, indicating by moving the door a little that Tam should get into the car.

She got in.

The door shut solidly and she heard him go around the back of the car to the other side and get in. She didn't look at the hands that started the car. She tried not to look at the hands that started the car. She tried not to look at the hand that shifted gears.

Automatically, expectantly, accustomed to hearing Barb's judgments, Tam listened for her voice as the car rolled quietly out of the parking lot. She didn't hear it.

five

Tam barely managed to sit still. She knew the enchantment would end soon, so she inhaled the magic, saving it for later, when she was alone again.

"A longer way home," he answered to the question she hadn't asked. "The night's too beautiful to waste." Stewart sounded reasonable—just a normal, handsome, elegant, sophisticated man who was driving her home in his little yellow convertible, the long way, because the night was too beautiful to waste.

Of course.

They cruised through the business district and round again. Gradually relaxing, she settled into the leather bucket seat, and lifted one hand to play with the air currents.

"You're smiling," he said at a light.

She nodded, "It's beautiful."

"Yes," he said.

She stole a glance at him. Was he real? Impossible.

As they pulled into Mrs. Warren's driveway, Tam said, "Thank you for bringing me home. But how did you know, I mean. . .Why did you offer me a ride?"

"You needed one."

"Yes, but why. . ."

"Luke sent me."

"That's all? You came because Luke sent you?"

"Yes."

She shut her eyes. To be picked up like a pound of liver—how humiliating! "Sorry," she said.

"Don't be," Stewart answered. "I enjoyed it. I'll be there tomorrow night."

She stared at him. "Tomorrow?"

"If you don't mind," he said.

He saw her fumble for the door handle and was out of the car and opening her door before she could connect with either handle or words. She struggled out of the car, too dazed to try floating.

"One thing, though," he said, holding her arm to steady her, "I open the doors. You just ride."

"Yes," she said obediently.

At her door he held out his hand. She looked at it.

"Key," he prompted.

"Yes," she said, forgetting "Thank you" and "Good night."

"Yes," she repeated later, alone.

Tomorrow. Maybe Luke had sent him this time, but Stewart had volunteered for tomorrow.

Why hadn't Luke come?

Strange. Everything about Luke was strange. An unpredictable presence, appearing and disappearing. Rescuing her in the night. Sending a ride. Almost as if he cared.

No. If he cared he'd have come himself. Never mind. Thanks to him, Stewart had come and this time she'd managed quite well. *Except for my looks*, she thought, remembering her droopy hair and worn cotton skirt. *He must think I'm a charity case. And my life is as drab my looks.*

Even a tiny sprinkling of stardust would help, she

thought, *and Stewart has enough glamour to share.*

She looked up at the attic window, thinking: *I know you're up there, Luke, painting in that turpentine t-shirt. With those giant hands. You sent your friend because you didn't want to take time to drive me home. Stay up there. I don't need you. You won't have to miss a single brush stroke.*

Suddenly she was angry—angry that he had sent Stewart, that Luke had seen her in the driveway and had taken her in his arms. Angry that he was there at all.

Next morning the van was gone; so was Stewart's convertible. Mrs. Warren was in her garden; Tam's tea and toast were on the table. Dad was on the porch, probably watching birds. She took her breakfast out to join him. He was sitting on the steps with small pieces of wood scattered about him, engrossed in sanding one edge. He didn't notice Tam until she spoke to him.

"Good morning, Dad. What're you doing?"

He looked more alive than he'd looked for a long time. His eyes lit up as he answered, "Making a bird feeder. We'll have more birds if we feed them regularly all seasons." His words flowed, enthusiastically, if not smoothly.

He showed her the floor, the three sides and the roof, which would be slanted when fastened to the walls. It would go on a pile among the backyard weeds.

She thought it was a terrific idea. Once he saw his creation surrounded by weeds, he might fix the mower. She didn't mention it.

He said, "I have to finish sanding before Luke gets home."

"What does Luke have to do with this?"

"It was his idea. . .his and mine," he said. "Luke says he'll come over after work. He's picking up paint on the way home. Red. House paint, not picture paint. Luke says. . ."

She listened to an hour of "Luke says. . .Luke says." She learned that Luke was working for Hoosier Tree Service, using skills he'd developed working in his uncle's landscaping business. The job provided enough to live on but left him free to do his real work, his painting. Because he wouldn't be climbing trees in bad weather, he could spend those days painting too.

Luke said he liked to work outdoors. That was funny, Tam said, considering that he spent every free second in the attic. Perhaps that was the reason, her father suggested. Perhaps his job was the only chance he had to see the outside. It made sense.

Luke said birds had to be fed all year round or they'd become accustomed to your feeder and then go hungry if you forgot them. Luke knew those things. He knew as many of the birds by name as Dad did and he knew more about their habits.

Luke said sunflower seeds were best for the birds in that area, especially for jays and chickadees.

Luke said. . . Luke said. . . Luke said. . .

Her father was full of what Luke said, full of the project and full of life. Two days ago she had despaired of a way to interest him. Luke had solved that problem.

She watched him on the porch, enjoying his enthusiasm, until she felt she had to get some work done. Inside the house, however, she was restless and kept returning to the porch. At last she brought the ironing board out on the porch so she could watch him while he worked. This gave her a kind of contentment.

By the time Tam went to work, the bird feeder was nearly put together. He'd have time to finish it and have his nap before Luke came. She hoped Luke remembered the paint. Maybe she could stop on the way to work somewhere. No. If she bought paint that would spoil the whole thing. She would leave that to Luke and her father.

Besides, she had other things to think about, like what to wear to work that would still look reasonably good after a night at Food Mart—good enough for the ride home with Stewart.

Nothing she owned looked good enough in the first place, much less after eight hours at work. It had been a long, long time since she'd worried about her looks.

Briefly, she considered taking along extra clothes to change into after work, but decided she couldn't appear in the parking lot with her Sunday dress on, carrying work clothes. He'd think she dressed up just for him. It would be true, but there was no point in advertising it.

Besides, he'd already seen her when she wasn't expecting him. She hadn't combed her hair or anything.

Remember, she cautioned herself, *this is nothing to Stewart. He's only a neighbor with a generous disposition, a neighbor who is doing his good deed for the day, or night. . . A neighbor who has a perfect smile, who. . .*

She had to do something with her hair.

She lifted one limp lock and let it drop. Hair spray wouldn't help. A hat, she thought. A wig? She pulled her hair back at the nape of her neck. Better. She'd wash and dry it before she left. It was the best she could do, she thought, and shrugged at her image in the mirror.

Later, clean and neat in starched blue blouse and dark

blue skirt, with sun-fluffed hair tied back with blue ribbon, she was as ready for work as she could get.

She planned to walk slowly, but once on the way, her feet moved faster and faster, hurrying to meet the evening. In spite of all her "slow walking," she was early to work. She knew her friends would put her starched, shiny look together with the handsome stranger in the parking lot. Wait till they saw him again tonight!

Be careful, she thought. *False hopes are a trap. Cinderella is for children. Convertibles and college and happily-ever-afters are for other people. When the fancy ride is over, I'll still be punching that time clock at three and eleven.* She'd enjoy this while it lasted and not hope for more.

I can do that, she thought, and wondered if she could.

Hope punched in, looked Tam over approvingly and said, "You look nice. I didn't know you knew the newcomer at church."

"Who?" Tam asked.

"Stewart. He was in church Sunday and Mr. Moore introduced him. I... didn't realize you knew him." Hope faltered on these last words, blushing.

"He's my new neighbor."

"Not bad, not bad," crowed Barbara, punching in. "Where did you find Prince Charming with the classy wheels?"

"Next door," Tam ventured cautiously.

"Next door! Then why haven't we seen him before?"

"He just moved in," Tam explained, keeping her answers minimal. Part of her wanted to bubble over with excitement and part of her wanted to keep it secret from Barbara so she wouldn't have to hear it every night for the next ten years. She'd tell the minimum and hope they wouldn't exaggerate simple kindness into a passionate love affair. Dealing with Barbara was never easy.

Barb was beginning already. "So this gorgeous hunk of man moved in and you never breathed a word about him to us. Some friend you are! The least you could do is let us know before he shows up so we could comb our hair. It's not every night we have a chance to watch you drive off with a movie star. I mean, there he was, smack in front of us, and you never breathed a word, not a word."

"I didn't know he was coming," Tam said. "It was a surprise."

"It sure was," Barb said. "And who's coming tonight?"

"He is."

"You're kidding," said Vickie. "He's coming here again tonight and you can stand there that cool? Aren't you even excited?"

Barb said, "She's excited, all right. Look how shiny bright she looks with her hair pulled back and her clothes all done up perfect. She's definitely excited. Come on, Tam; what's the story?

"No story. Honest. Of course I dressed up the best I could. Wouldn't you? But to Stewart I'm just a neighbor who needs a ride. That's all."

"That's his name? Stewart?" asked Vickie.

"Stewart," said Barb, considering it.

"Stewie," simpered Vickie.

"Don't," Tam said. "Just don't. Nothing like this has happened to me for years. Please. Be my friends. Don't spoil it for me."

Vickie looked to Barb for direction. At Tam's back she could feel Hope watching. At last Barb said, "Okay, if that's the way you want it."

Tam nodded.

They were busy that night, but not too busy to joke back and forth. Hope, working in back, wasn't included, but the tension of the coffee incident was over, set aside to maintain good working relationships.

At break they sat on the edge of the loading platform as always—Vickie, Barb, and Tam, with Hope several feet to Tam's left. It might have been any other night in the last few weeks except that things lay between them now that made them uneasy with each other.

Neither Barb nor Vickie would mention those items that went home in the pockets of their smocks, not in front of Hope. Tam didn't think Barb had told Vickie they'd quarreled. Vickie was no good at keeping secrets; she'd have said something if she'd known.

Hope hadn't confronted Barb about the coffee machine, and Barb hadn't apologized. They went on, pretending nothing had happened. The one change was that Barb was letting Hope alone. She wasn't exactly pleasant to her, but she wasn't badgering her either. Tam wondered if this would be the new pattern of their relationship or whether Barb return to annoying Hope after the caution wore off. Either way it was an improvement.

"You look nice," Barb ventured. "Blue is good on you."

"Thanks," Tam said, grateful for easy conversation. "I had trouble finding something that looks good."

"Your hair is better that way too," Barb said.

"I can't do anything with it. It just hangs there like ears on a hound."

Barb suggested, "You'd look cute with short hair. Why don't I cut it? I cut my daughter's hair all the time, and my sister's too. I can do it."

"I don't think so."

"Why not?"

"Vickie, don't you think Tam would look cute with short hair?" Barb leaned back so Vickie could study Tam's hair and come up with the opinion Barb had already given her.

"You'd look good with short hair," said Vickie.

"See?" said Barb.

With Barb's talk of the best style and when and where to cut, Tam felt she barely managed to escape the break with hair still on her head. She promised to think it over, which was as far as she was willing to go with the idea.

It was nice of Barb to want to help, though, thought Tam. Barb could be a good friend when she wanted to be.

On their way back to checkout, Mack stopped to ask if Mr. Brill had been in since Tam had jumped out of his car. He hadn't. Barb said she didn't think he'd have the nerve to show up after that, but Mack didn't agree.

"He'll be back," he said, "and when he comes in, I want to speak to him. I can't have him scaring my help like that. You let me know right away when he comes in."

They promised. *Another friend,* Tam thought. *He may be primarily concerned about his groceries, but he's trying to protect me.* She wondered what Mack would say to Mr. Brill if he ever did come in, which he wouldn't.

Because they were busy after break, Tam didn't start watching the clock until almost nine. Once she did start, the time crawled by. She checked the clock after each customer. At ten she began keeping one eye on the entrance, just in case Mrs. Warren wanted Stewart to pick up some cereal or something, since he was going to the grocery anyway.

At ten thirty she began watching the cars in the

parking lot.

Her unreliable stomach was beginning to twist and her hands were cold. The register keys played tricks on her; she made mistakes she'd never made before, not even when she was first learning how to use the register. Her knees felt watery and she grew clumsy. If eleven did not come soon, she would break a bottle or drop eggs or squash grapes or bounce a bag of flour off her foot.

It was a very long half hour. At the end of it, at eleven, no little yellow car sat outside the door.

Tam tried to tell herself she was glad. She was a nervous wreck and was relieved no handsome Stewart was there to see her disintegrate behind the counter. She was also disappointed.

She told herself it was all right that he had forgotten to appear, that it wasn't really important, that she could get home alone. She told herself that, but she didn't believe it.

Barb and Vickie dawdled with their cash drawers, hanging around in front so they could see Stewart drive up. In the back room Tam freshened up the best she could, combing her hair and brushing her teeth with the toothbrush she had brought in her purse.

He's not there, she thought, *but I might as well do the best I can, just in case.* She tried to look nonchalant as she hung up her smock, but her eyes met Hope's and they both knew Tam was not calm at all.

"He's here!" croaked Barb in a hoarse whisper. She and Vickie dashed into the back room. "He's here! Let's see how you look." She straightened Tam's collar in the back. "Not bad, kid." She gave Tam's hair a quick pat and pushed her toward the door.

"Wait! I forgot to punch out," Tam cried.

"I'll do it," said Barb. "Get going."

Tam went.

six

In the softness of the lovely evening. Tam's head and heart betrayed her. She no longer had to concentrate to seem to float on air. She floated without aid or effort, lighter than the evening air that whispered through her idle fingers.

This second of many rides home was the beginning of a dream life. At first she felt like a stranger in this magical world of romance, but she soon adapted. Before too many rides she began to feel a part of it, as unreal as the rest of the setting. Each night at eleven she stepped from paper bags and potatoes into stardust and sophistication. By twelve she stepped out of the dream and into the dim kitchen.

She agreed to the haircut on the condition that Barb forget movie stars and keep the cut simple. Barb agreed, so early Saturday morning Barb came to cut, shampoo, and set.

...And to catch a close-up, "accidental" look at Stewart. Barb was disappointed. Stewart, and Luke, were gone.

Barb was drying Tam's hair in the sun, coaxing it into waves, when Mrs. Warren came to inspect the little red-roofed bird feeder high on its metal pipe pole in the weeds. She pronounced it just the thing. Luke said she would like it and she did. Luke also said Dad might make her one.

Luke said. Luke said.

Mrs. Warren asked, as usual, if Tam intended to attend church the next day. She was used to evasive answers, but

84

Tam's determined "Yes" surprised and pleased her.

"Just church, Mrs. Warren, not Sunday school."

"Whatever you say, dear."

Tam didn't admit that she was motivated primarily by curiosity about what Hope drew from church. If Tam had, Mrs. Warren would have discussed it, which Tam didn't want. She wanted to see for herself.

Mrs. Warren didn't mention Stewart. Tam thought that, for a woman who loved to talk, Mrs. Warren had been exceptionally closed-mouthed recently. Mrs. Warren might think Stewart was the reason Tam was going, but she didn't say so. *Good,* thought Tam. *Maybe Mrs. Warren won't send Stewart over for me on Sunday morning.*

Telling Mrs. Warren she wasn't going to Sunday school should stop that. Mrs. Warren always went to Sunday school and surely would take "the boys" with her.

"Who's Luke?" asked Barb, when Mrs. Warren had gone.

"The other neighbor," Tam said. "Nobody special."

"That's what you said about Stewart," said Barb.

Tam shrugged.

In less than an hour, Tam's hair was dry, Barb was gone, and Mrs. Warren was inspecting the results, claiming the hair was "a picture, an absolute picture."

Mrs. Warren stood watching Dad mark out the bird feeder pattern on the scraps of wood and then announced —too casually—that she and "the boys" would like Tam and her father to join them for Sunday dinner.

"No," said Dad.

"Fine," said Mrs. Warren. "Come over right after you get home from church."

Dad blinked at Tam in surprise, wondering when he had

decided to go to church. Tam smiled as if to say there was nothing she could do about it now that Mrs. Warren had made up her mind. He raised his eyebrows but didn't argue. Tam hoped he'd be as cooperative in the morning.

At noon Mrs. Warren was back, this time with a dress, still in its plastic cleaner's bag. "Would you do me a favor, dear?" she asked.

She'd found this old dress when she cleaned out the attic for Luke. Well, actually it was almost new. Anyway, it didn't fit her and there was no use pretending she'd lose enough weight to wear it, especially since it was too tight when she bought it. But it was too good to waste— real silk—no good to anybody in the attic. All it did was take up room. A real shame, considering how much she had paid for it.

"Would you mind trying it on to see if you could get a little use out of it? As a favor?"

Tam knew Mrs. Warren was only slightly larger than she, but arguing was impossible, especially since Tam didn't try very hard.

The dress was the most beautiful garment she'd touched in years, possibly in her whole life. It slid on smoothly and hung evenly at exactly the right length, as if made for Tam. The soft rose-pink added color to her face and softened the shadows around her eyes. When she moved, it moved with her, whispering lightly as a sigh as she turned this way and that in front of her mirror.

Silk.

Tam wriggled her shoulders against the downy fabric. "Are you sure?" she asked.

"Sure as sure, honey," Mrs. Warren said. "It was your dress all along. I just didn't know it till now."

"I'll wear it to church," promised Tam.

"Yes, and to my house for dinner." Mrs. Warren kissed Tam lightly on the cheek and left her admiring herself in the mirror.

The day had flown by and so did the night. The haircut was a great success. Everybody at work liked it, even Mack. She loved the approval in Stewart's eyes as he said, "Nice haircut."

Sunday morning, with her new haircut and rose-petal dress, Tamara looked younger and softer than she had dared to hope. She was up and dressed early, and Dad was in a good mood. He wore his blue blazer and his white shoes, matching her with a snappy look of his own.

They were early enough to secure a back seat. She knew her father would go home rather than sit up front.

The organist was playing something subdued in what the bulletin said was "time to sit quietly in our pews and prepare our hearts for worship." Tam found this difficult. People kept stopping to speak to her or to Dad.

You'd think we haven't been here for years, Tam thought. *We were here just . . . Easter. Oh.*

The big welcome was embarrassing but warming. Dad's first responses were stand-offish and brusque, but he rapidly relaxed.

Hope came in, looked around for Tam, smiled delightedly, and came directly over. Tam introduced Hope to Dad, who offered to move over so she could join them.

Tam said quickly, "Hope always sits in the front. She says she likes to be surrounded by the singing."

"That's all right," Hope said. "I'd rather sit with you."

Dad urged Tam to sit with her up front, but Tam was not persuaded until Mrs. Warren appeared, followed by

Stewart, smiling in Sunday perfection, and Luke. Tam waited to greet them before going to sit up front, watching and pretending not to watch for Stewart's reaction. She needn't have worried.

His smile radiated over all three of them. He lingered briefly over Hope's hand when he shook it and seemed to have difficulty breaking eye contact with Hope. His natural charm, Tam thought, noting that his impact on Hope was as forceful as it had been on her. Hope was blushing, visibly flustered by his touch.

He must be used to that, she thought. *My own awkwardness must have seemed quite normal to him. He might even miss it if it were not there.* She repressed a giggle and looked away to hide it. . .

Right into the knowing brown eyes of Luke.

Waiting to be introduced, he observed Stewart's charm and Hope's confusion, then focused on Tam. She knew she might have hidden her laughter from the others, but not from him.

His slightly puzzled frown pleased Tam, who liked knowing he couldn't read *every* wrinkle in her brain.

Perhaps he was puzzled that she hadn't seemed jealous or possessive when Stewart charmed Hope. If so, Luke was forgetting two things: Stewart wasn't seriously interested in her, and Stewart couldn't help being charming.

He is what he is, thought Tam. *Surely Luke knows that.*

Mrs. Warren introduced Luke to Hope and it was Tam's turn to observe reactions. Too well she knew the strength of Luke's hand, the power it had to melt her bones. As Hope's meeting with Stewart had echoed Tam's own, so Hope's meeting with Luke would confirm Tam's response to his strength. Tam waited for the fluttering that would give Hope away.

She didn't flutter. They shook hands and exchanged How-do-you-do's and smiled. Tam saw nothing of that weakness that had washed over her when. . .

It wasn't the same. Shaking hands in the aisle of the church wasn't the same as being swept up in his arms in the rainy night shadows. If Hope had been there, thought Tam, she'd have felt it too.

Hope's gaze remained on Stewart and his on her. Tam shifted uncomfortably from one foot to the other, knowing Luke was studying her again, this time with a trace of anger in his face—anger mixed with something unidentifiable. Concern?

Perhaps.

"Let's sit," Luke said gruffly, pushing Stewart into the pew across from Dad and sliding in after him, leaving Mrs. Warren to sit with Dad. Hope and Tam settled in the fifth row, far in front, just in time for the Call to Worship.

Tam's mind was miles away from hymns and prayers. No, not miles. A few rows. She scarcely heard the opening of the service or the first hymn.

Next to her, Hope's voice—sweet, clear, young—rose in light soprano with the worshipers, and Tam wondered again what Hope found here.

Tam listened for it, watched for it, but didn't find it. Church was like it always was—pleasant, but not the answer to her question.

For Tam the best part was the stained glass window which filled the entire right wall of the sanctuary. In high school, she had asked Mr. Simms, their pastor then, about the window and learned it was called "The Road to

Emmaus" and that it was about a place where Jesus had walked with two of His followers after He had risen from the grave.

Jesus's friends hadn't recognized Him, Mr. Simms had explained. They walked and talked with Him, but didn't know Him. Not until later, when Jesus had opened their eyes to Him, did they know Him.

As it had a hundred times before, Tam's imagination wandered down the Road to Emmaus on the caramel glass between leaded trees and the milky blue of the stream.

She wondered what it was like to meet Him on the road and whether she'd have recognized Him. When she was younger she was sure she'd have known Him instantly. Now she thought not. If His close friends failed to know Him, why would she?

Would Jesus have walked with me? she wondered. He had walked with two who were His followers, two Christians. Tam was Christian. She'd always considered herself Christian, anyway, even though Barb said no one would ever guess it.

With Hope it was no secret. Her faith was one of the first things people noticed about her. They might not always like it, but they noticed. It was so much a part of her that it was impossible to imagine her any other way. It just sort of radiated from her.

Am I a Christian? She knew the answer was no. Not like that.

Hope pulled at Tam's elbow for her to rise and Tam realized that the congregation was singing. She followed the words in the book Hope held, but did not sing.

She bowed her head for the closing prayer and the benediction, but she did not pray. She was on the Road to

Emmaus.

Slowly becoming aware that people were filing out, Tam edged into the aisle, followed by Hope, who breathed, "Wasn't it wonderful?"

"I. . ." Tam struggled for words, but none came.

"What is it?" Hope asked.

Above her head "The Road to Emmaus" glowed rich with sunlight. Tam shook her head. *She might understand,* Tam thought, *if I could explain. Then she might answer my question.*

Some other time, Tam thought, *when I have the words.*

Then Tam felt sudden empathy for Dad, a glimmer of understanding of his inability to find words, of being able to feel but not able to express the feeling.

She looked for him where she had left him, but he was gone. Slipped out a little early, as usual, she guessed. Crowds frightened him since the stroke. He worried about being to able to get out fast if he felt ill. He probably was already outside.

Tam glanced at the back aisle to be certain, and found her eyes locked again with Luke's.

Stunned momentarily by the contact, she didn't notice that Stewart had pushed through the crowd and was almost next to her. His voice close to her ear startled her and she jumped guiltily, breaking the link with Luke.

"You're dreaming, Tam," Stewart joked. "You're not used to getting up so early."

She had no clever answer, so she just shrugged.

Stewart moved between Hope and Tam, steering them up the aisle with a hand on the shoulder of each. Tam banged against a pew, driven into it by Stewart, who was trying to crowd three across a two-person aisle. Absently she shook

his hand from her shoulder and moved a little ahead,
leaving him to steer Hope.

Hope apparently liked the arrangement and would have
continued that way if Luke hadn't pushed into the aisle
next to her. His huge shoulders were too much for Stewart,
whose hand was jostled off Hope's shoulder as Luke
forced him ahead of Hope and next to Tam. It looked like
natural casual jostling, the way Luke intended it to look.

Hope was still with Luke when they gathered outside to
walk home together, so naturally Mrs. Warren asked her
to join them for dinner. Hope accepted eagerly and chatted
easily with Mrs. Warren as the group paraded two by two
to Mrs. Warren's house. Next to Tam, Dad was quiet but
in good spirits. The boys, last, were silent, but Tam felt
their presence and was glad to be wearing the lovely silk
dress.

Mrs. Warren had gone all out to produce one of her
famous dinners. Not one of those chilly affairs with finger
bowls and place cards, it was a dinner like the ones she had
prepared for her husband and children.

In spite of the heat, she served roast beef, dark brown and
fork-tender, with mashed potatoes and gravy, green beans
from her garden, biscuits with her own peach jam, and an
extravagant gelatin salad with whipped cream and fruit
and baby marshmallows. At the foot of the table she
smoothed her hands over her apron and beamed at them
over her grandmother's cut-glass pitcher.

At the head of the table, across shared joys and sorrows,
Tam's father smiled back. Mrs. Warren nodded to him,
but he shook his head almost imperceptibly, so she asked
Luke to say grace. She knew, of course, that Dad wouldn't
risk praying aloud in front of the group, but asking him told

him the choice was his.

Luke's voice was deep and rich as he gave thanks for God's blessing. His prayer was simple, not elaborate, the prayer of a man with a close relationship with God. What was it that marked these people, made them special?

Dinner was clatter of forks, chatter, and laughter—Thanksgiving Day in midsummer, without the stress of the holiday season. They set in with good appetite, especially the boys, and did justice to the feast.

When all declared they couldn't eat another bite, not another bite, Mrs. Warren brought the blackberry cobbler, still warm from the oven, and vanilla ice cream to go on top. They found that they could, after all, eat just a little more.

After that they groaned and moaned and held their stomachs, declaring they were too full to move and wouldn't have to eat again for a month.

Satisfied, Mrs. Warren passed the great old family Bible over to Luke, who read a chapter from Romans before closing with prayer, officially ending dinner.

When Mrs. Warren rose to begin clearing the table, the younger guests insisted that she and Dad rest while they did dishes. Mrs. Warren and Dad retired to the front porch swing, where the regular squeak of the swinging chains against their ceiling hooks announced that all was well.

The dishes dirtied by only six eaters were enough to have fed Tam and Dad for a week. Tam washed. The others took turns drying and putting away.

They were all the way down to the roaster and the cobbler dish when Mrs. Warren reminded Tam that it was time to go to work.

Tam had forgotten.

"Oh dear," she said, snatching up the cobbler dish. "I've got to hurry. What about you, Hope?"

"I don't work Sundays," Hope said.

"Oh, yes, that's right. Well, I do, and I have only thirty-five minutes to get there," Tam said.

Luke pushed her away from the sink, taking the cobbler dish from her hands. "I'll finish this," he said. "You get ready. Stewart will take you to work. Right, Stew?"

"Right."

Tam dried her hands and ran. At home she pulled the silken dress over her head and laid it carefully on the bed. She popped on the first clean skirt she found and topped it with a crisp white blouse, then turned to the mirror to run a comb through her short hair. Ready.

Outside, Stewart was holding the car door open. Even in a rush, he did things gracefully. As he shut the door, Tam said, "You don't have to do this, but I'm glad you are. I don't want to be late. I need that job."

"It's a pleasure," Stewart responded. "For a girl who looked as lovely as you did in that pink dress, I'd drive across town anytime."

"Thank you," she said.

"You don't really need that job, you know," he said. "You could get another one that isn't so exhausting, one with better hours. Why do you stay there?"

Tam never had given it much thought. Whenever she thought of the job, she was glad to have it. She hadn't wanted to spend her life in the grocery, but an art career was impossible. Without that, one job was as good as another.

She didn't explain that, saying honestly that it was the only job she knew how to do, that she had no other skills.

"Learn to type," he said, "or to do computer programming."

"That costs money," she answered, "and I'd have to go to school at night to learn. I work at night."

He nodded. "I see what you mean. We'll have to think this over."

"We?"

"You and I," he explained, "and Luke, of course."

"What does Luke have to do with me and my job?"

"Nothing. It's just that Luke always knows what to do. If it hadn't been for Luke I'd have been lying dead in the middle of nowhere and no one the wiser. He pulled me out of there and saved my life. He's the one who knew I would do well in business administration and helped me get started. He was right, too. I'm happy with my job and my employers are happy with me. Luke says. . . ."

"Luke says, Luke says," Tam objected impatiently. "That's all I hear. What's so wonderful about Luke that every word he says has to quoted?"

Stewart turned to her with raised eyebrows and an astonishment that almost immediately gave way to amusement. He chuckled softly. "Luke said you had a temper."

"Aarrrgh!!!" Her growl drew Stewart's laughter. Scootching low in the seat, she barricaded herself with folded arms and glowered at the dashboard.

These arrogant men with their lives grasped firmly in their hands were beginning to annoy her. They imagined that all she had to do was decide to have a new life and a new life would happen.

They didn't know about giving up dreams. They hadn't sat hours with a father who was clinging to remnants of his self-respect. They didn't know how quickly the little security she had managed could evaporate in sudden illness or a lost job.

Tam knew. She knew the job market was almost zero for people with limited experience and no skills. She also knew that she couldn't afford to be unemployed while she sought a new career.

Stewart with his fine job and Luke with his eternal painting had no one but themselves to spend their money on. She would have to be careful, she thought. These people could put grand ideas in her head, make her long for things she could never have, make her lose what little she had. Glamour and romance were fine, but they weren't enough to live on.

What I should do, if I have any sense at all, she thought, *is stay away from Stewart. One day he'll find a new neighbor to feel sorry for and I'll be left with nothing but a broken heart and a set of overgrown expectations.*

She didn't want to stay away from Stewart. That was the problem. If this was all her future held, she wanted it. When he left, she would still have memories. It was better than nothing.

The trick was to let her head float above the clouds, but keep her feet firmly on earth. Not so easy. She wasn't sure she could do it.

"We're here." Stewart's voice broke through to her and she raised her head to see the orange and blue Food Mart sign directly in front of the car. She turned to thank him, but he was already out and standing by her open door, waiting.

She wondered how long she had sat engrossed in her own thoughts. She thought she saw amusement in his eyes, but when she looked more sharply, it was gone.

Thanking him quickly, she dashed in the front entrance, entirely forgetting that Mack wanted them to use the back one during daylight hour. She never did that, never did the unusual. Day after day, night after night, Tam's comings and goings were regulated by the clock, steady, dependable. Dull. Not the way she'd been acting lately.

Once she punched in, the rudeness of her behavior in the car hit her. What had she done? Stewart was interested, trying to help. She should have been grateful, or at least civil. Instead she had snapped at him and quarreled. She had been rude without excuse. Why was she being so disagreeable?

It was that "Luke said" business that set me off, she thought. Every time I turn around it's "Luke said." He is definitely getting on my nerves.

Why? He hadn't done anything to her. She had barely spoken with him since that first night.

Dad saw him, often, when she was not home. They worked on bird feeders and discussed sunflower seeds and all kinds of things.

Mrs. Warren saw him enough to begin to depend on him. She had asked Luke, not Stewart, to ask the blessing at dinner.

Stewart saw him. Everybody saw him but Tam.

You would think, wouldn't you, she fumed, that after he carried me from the driveway and patched up my hands . . .and knees. . . .and saw me safely home. . . .

You would think that the next time I saw him he would at least be friendly instead of acting like we've never met. He scarcely spoke to me, never once mentioned that night.

At dinner he had been quieter than the others except where Hope was involved. He was always quick to sit next

*to her, walk next to her, talk with her. You would think the
only person in the place was Hope, that I didn't exist.*

Expect that now and then, when Tam wasn't expecting
it, she had met his eyes by accident. It was unnerving, that
steady look of his. It confused her. It almost frightened
her, but not really. It wasn't that kind of look. It was a kind
of concerned interest, guarded, but knowing.

She couldn't decide what to make of it. She did know,
however, that Luke was an infuriating, frustrating, annoying man. A mere mention of his name set her teeth on edge.

Nonsense, she thought. Luke is a man who lives next
door. Their meeting was accidental and unimportant to
him, except as an embarrassment he preferred not to
mention.

Tam could understand that. She felt the same way here
at work sometimes. Moreover, from what he had seen of
her, she was sure he found her childish and tiresome.

More childish than Hope? Evidently. Absolutely. She
guessed she couldn't blame him.

Nevertheless, Luke was Stewart's friend. To get along
with Stewart she would have to get along with Luke. She
also was reluctant to cause any trouble between Dad and
his new friend. That would be cruel.

She would get along with him, that's all, and be nice
about it. It wouldn't be difficult, considering how rarely
she saw him. And she would have to apologize to Stewart.

With all this on her mind, she was in no mood to joke and
play or be around others who were lively. She felt itchy,
wriggly, snappish. To Barb's hints about her ill-tempered
distance, she was unresponsive and even more distant.

Nothing went right. They were busy, but she wanted to
be alone. She found conversation an irritation, but every

customer was chatty. Barb was in one of her easy-going, funny moods; Tam had no patience.

The conveyer belt had a nasty habit of moving when she pressed the foot control, even though she didn't intend to press the control. The lights all worked for a change, so the light seemed glaring. Mack was nosy, hanging around, keeping an eye on everything. Nothing went right.

At six Mack pulled her off checkout and put her to sorting good strawberries from bad and she retired to the relative seclusion of the produce department. Relieved, she set in with a will, applying stifled energies to the simple task of creating clean, attractive baskets full of good berries.

That's where Mr. Brill found her.

He crept up behind her from the other side of the potatoes before she realized anyone was there. He took the plastic basket from her hands and clasped them in his, looking soulfully into her eyes.

"Tam," he whispered, "why did you leave me like that?"

"Let me go," Tam demanded, pulling back.

He was stronger than he looked. Holding her hands firmly, he whispered, "I can't let you go. I've searched for you all my life. You belong to me."

"I'll scream."

"No, you won't scream. You know that I'm your friend." He smiled sweetly, close to her face.

"Mack!" The cry came from inside her before she realized it existed. "Mack!" she shouted again.

"Why did you do that?" whimpered Mr. Brill, squeezing her hands tightly. "Why did you do that?"

Then Mack was there and so was Al, and between them they opened Mr. Brill's grasp and released her. Mack led Mr. Brill away to the office, talking quietly to him. Al held onto his other arm, his height ensuring that Mr. Brill cooperated. Mr. Brill looked small between them, and helpless. Poor little man. Tam felt sorry for him.

Far away, at the other end of the aisle, Tam saw Mack pick up the telephone, tap the number buttons, and talk briefly into the receiver. Interesting, but not important. She was calm, glassy calm. She stood absolutely still next to the mound of strawberries, calm. Mack cast a worried glance in her direction and shouted for Barbara.

Tam smiled vaguely. *Mack must think I need help or comfort, but I don't. He must expect me to be upset, to break into tears or have hysterics or something, but I won't. None of this is important.*

She was absolutely calm.

When the police arrived to question her about the incident, she patiently told them what had happened. They and Mr. Brill seemed to know each other. They left with poor little Mr. Brill in the back of their squad car. He looked lost, alone.

"Are you all right?" Barb asked.

"Fine."

"Why don't you take a break? Mack will let you go home early. Let me call you a cab."

"I'm fine," Tam repeated.

"Don't you want to rest a while?"

"I'm fine," Tam said, and mechanically picked up the basket Mr. Brill had taken from her. She saw the worried looks Barb and Mack exchanged, but the looks meant nothing.

Mack said something about calling Tam's father, but it was not important. It didn't penetrate her perfect calm. She went back to her sorting: good berry in the basket, rotten berry in the box, good berry, rotten berry. . .

Luke?

Luke was there. How odd. And he was very angry. Scowling. He brushed the berries away like sand from a child's hands. She regarded him placidly. His scowl deepened.

Grasping her firmly with one arm round her shoulders and taking her purse from Barbara, he maneuvered Tam through the store and out the front. She went passively along, although she knew Mack would want her to use the back door.

In the parking lot Luke stuffed her unceremoniously into his van and jerked into gear. He drove home in angry silence and Tam had nothing to say either.

Dad was in the driveway and so was Mrs. Warren, who hustled Tam into her own room and into nightgown and robe. A rattle of dishes from the kitchen told Tam Dad was making tea. Tam observed this from another dimension. It was not important.

On the bed where she had laid it after the dinner was the glorious pink silk dress. Tam drifted over to it and ran her hand across its softness. Holding it up to her robe, she swayed a little, feeling the silk follow her movement. Lovely, she crooned to herself. Lovely She turned to the mirror to dream in the reflection. She spread the skirt, holding one fold so that the fullness of the fabric floated when she moved.

Lovely.

Something was on it, some bit of fluff or thread. She brushed at it with the back of her hand but it remained. She leaned closer to the light and held up the offending spot for closer inspection. The dark gray-blue smear would not brush off. She rubbed but it remained. Stubborn, she thought. What was it? She held it closer to the light and rubbed again.

Blackberry.

Please, not blackberry. It would never come out.

"No," she wailed, "not my new dress. Please not my new dress."

She sank to the bed, pressing her delicate pink silk to her heart and sobbing for all she was worth.

"Now, now," soothed Mrs. Warren, hurrying in from the kitchen to cradle Tam in her arms, but it did no good. Tam's tears, once started, would not stop, until she cried herself to sleep.

seven

Dark. Tam squinted at the luminous dial of her clock radio. Three o'clock. Groan. Her head hurt as she sat up and threw off the clinging sheet. She rolled forward to lie with her head in the cool breeze at the foot of the bed and gazed out at the night.

Luke's attic light was on. She pictured him up there, painting, scowling. With sudden pain she remembered the evening and sat up again, abruptly, then sank back to the pillow. *Poor Mr. Brill,* she thought. *And poor Luke—always having to rescue me from one scrape or another. No wonder he avoids me.*

He'd seen her looking normal only one day—at church and at the dinner, in that lovely silk. . .

Blackberry stain. She remembered that now too, and the flood of tears that followed the discovery. *Strange,* she thought, *I was calm with Mr. Brill but not with the stain. I must have upset Dad.*

She went to see if he was all right, gliding along in the unlit house with ease born of a lifetime of familiarity.

He was awake. Over tea in the kitchen, she told him about Mr. Brill and that eerie calm she had felt. Shock, he decided, which explained her over-reaction to the stain. That was a shame, they agreed, but it wasn't worth tears.

Tam nodded, thinking, *It's the way I am—calm in disaster. Later, I fall apart.*

The night Dad had his stroke she had sat waiting calmly

in the hospital. Later, at home, alone, tears came.

Jumping out of Mr. Brill's car was less serious, but it was the same pattern. She was scared out there in the bushes, but she kept her wits all the way home. Then, when she knew she was safe, she fell.

It's a good way to be, she supposed, except since no one saw the lonely tears, no one suspected how dearly she paid for the calm. Other girls cried or fainted; Tam coped. She saw no choice, no one to lean on.

Except Dad, of course, but she was careful not to upset him. Mrs. Warren was always willing to help, but she was a neighbor and friend, not family, not someone whose love made him part of her.

Sometimes Tam had lain awake at night, imagining that Robert still cared and returned to hold her close and protect her, folding his arms around her, saying "Lean on me." Robert couldn't have prevented the trouble, but his understanding would have helped.

Seeing other people's lives were easier and that public weepers got more sympathy had made her resent the injustice. Then, realizing that "unfair" is for children, she began to suspect that she wasn't the only person carrying a burden in silence. Others around her must also be struggling alone. She grew more sensitive to others' pain, finding it in Barb, in Mrs. Warren, in Dad, and took comfort from knowing that if they were managing, she could.

How silly to cry over a dress, Tam thought. *I can cope with that. Tomorrow. And Dad? Luke had told him not to worry.*

Luke said. . .

His light still burned when Tam finally returned to bed.

She found that curiously comforting. She would thank
Luke when she saw him, if she ever saw him.

For a second or two she considered throwing pebbles at
his window again to speak to him. She couldn't run out in
the driveway at four o'clock in the morning in her nightgown and throw pebbles at the neighbor's window! What
was she thinking of?

She shut her mind and went to sleep, waking to a normal
Monday morning.

Mr. Brill lurked in the fringes of Tam's mind, as fright-
ening in daylight as he was that night in the car. Tam pitied
him, but he scared her. He was stronger than he looked,
and more determined. Worse, there was no telling what
he would do next. She tried not to think about him.

While Dad counted birds, Tam inspected the ruined silk
dress, hooking the hanger over the top of the open kitchen
door where the light was best. Could it be washed?

She thought so, but would the stain get better? or worse?
She tried washing just the stained section of the skirt with
mild soap, then stronger soap. No good. The stain
lightened a smidgen and changed from blue-gray to gray
and the pink was fading too.

She quit. She toweled it dryish and rehung it in the
doorway, a sad, limp little dress.

Ruined, she thought. Give up. But she couldn't. Even
ruined it was the loveliest thing she owned. She would
hang it in her closet, royalty among the cottons, to look at
and caress occasionally. As it moved in the breeze she
remembered how it had felt—like a flower petal.

Mrs. Warren brushed past it when she came in. How was
Tam today, she wanted to know, and how was Dad, and
what could she do to help, and here was a little salad for

lunch. When Mrs. Warren thought of comfort and support, she thought of food.

Mrs. Warren turned to the miserable-looking silk. "What are you going to do with it?"

"Hang it in the closet," said Tam, "unless you have a better idea."

"Well," said Mrs. Warren, "once we covered a hole in my Sally's dress with a big flower—sewed it on like a patch. Looked liked it belonged there."

"Not in the middle of the skirt, though," Tam pointed out. "And not that big."

"No. You can't go around with a bouquet stuck on the front of your skirt. Too heavy. Must be something you could put there to cover it up. A little ruffled apron, maybe. A pocket?"

"A coat?" Tam suggested.

"Don't be fresh, Tamara," Mrs. Warren said, laughing. "Too bad it's plain pink. If the fabric had flowers all over it, the spot wouldn't show so bad."

"Flowers all over. That's it!" Tam cried.

"Too heavy."

"Not if they're painted on."

Mrs. Warren spread the skirt, trying to picture flowers. Her slow tentative nod grew into enthusiasm. It was exactly her kind of crazy idea.

They needed paints. Tam had some, someplace, but where?

In the last place she looked, of course—on the top shelf of the coat closet, under postcards her mother had saved. The brushes were stiff, but could be softened with turpentine, if it hadn't evaporated. The paints were hard in tubes that cracked when Tam squeezed them. The linseed oil was yellow and sticky. The palette was still good, though, and clean. She'd use Dad's turpentine and make do with the rest.

Mrs. Warren washed the dress free of dry cleaning chemicals and ironed it dry in little more than an hour. She arranged it on the super-clean kitchen table, putting newspaper inside to separate front from back so paint wouldn't soak through to the back.

With mounting excitement, Tam mixed the paints on the palette. Flowers, she thought, soft and floating colors for a soft and floating dress. Rose and greens. A touch of lavender for balance. Gray to blend into the gray stain.

Humming, she blended the colors in different strengths and combinations, adding a little white here, a little cadmium red there. When she was satisfied, she thinned them with turpentine so they would flow on easily. Turpentine would make it dry faster, too.

Filling her widest brush with the lightest of the colors and taking a deep breath, echoed by Mrs. Warren, Tam touched the brush to the edge of the stain and stroked it lightly across the silk. The color stayed where she put it, almost transparent in its thin solution, but firm enough to cover the color of the skirt.

The first stroke was the hardest. After that she relaxed, humming as she worked.

Loose, soft-edged flowers appeared under her hand and spread themselves across the skirt diagonally up to the waist. From there they flourished across the bodice and up to the left shoulder. It was tempting to go on making flowers up the other side and down the back and on the sleeves, but Tam stopped.

"What do you think?" she asked Mrs. Warren.

"Lovely," Mrs. Warren breathed softly. "No one would ever know. It's better than it was before."

"It needs a sprinkle of white for contrast, and maybe a line or two of black," Tam mused, and picked up a finer brush, to add the delicate touches. "There."

"Lovely," repeated Mrs. Warren. "I have a white silk blouse. Do you think you could. . ."

"Of course. Right now, before I put the paint away."

Tam used Mrs. Warren's kitchen table for the blouse, so both blouse and dress could lie undisturbed to dry. When it was done, they surveyed the morning's work with satisfaction, pleased with themselves and the results.

"You were humming while you worked," said Mrs. Warren. "You did that when you were little, but I haven't heard you do it lately."

"I haven't been this happy for a long time," Tam said. "I forgot how much I enjoy painting."

"You ought to take it up again."

"I don't have much time for things like this."

"No, I suppose you don't. It's a shame to waste all that talent." Mrs. Warren shook her head.

Tam and Dad ate on the back porch because the kitchen table was covered by the dress.

"Those weeds are getting pretty high," Tam said.

Dad shook his head. "No. Butterfly garden." He pointed to a flash of yellow fluttering near the pole. "Luke says. . ."

Luke again. He had convinced Dad not to cut the weeds, explaining that butterflies thrive on weeds and need them for home and food. They like variety and depend most heavily on the very weeds Tam was trying to eliminate—goldenrod, clover, thistles, ragweed, dandelion. They are especially fond of small, simple flowers like the daisies, phlox, petunias, and alyssum in Mrs. Warren's garden.

Furthermore, butterflies need nearby bushes, like the hedge across the back of the yard, and trees. They would love the willow behind the garage. The back yard was a perfect butterfly garden, Luke said.

"There's no such thing," Tam argued.

"No," Dad argued back, nodding his head yes.

Luke said Winston Churchill had had one at his estate to show off to tell visitors. Churchill had even stocked it with more impressive specimens when he was expecting more impressive guests.

Churchill and Luke were too much for Tam. She might as well accept the butterfly garden and forget about cutting weeds.

Tam hoped Luke had told Mrs. Warren about the butterflies. Tam was sure Mrs. Warren didn't consider the weeds beautiful and didn't view her flowers as dessert. If Luke said it, though, Mrs. Warren would approve.

Two young squirrels chased and wrestled, and Tam laughed to see them scramble up and down the pole, stumbling onto the birds' sunflower seeds. A bonanza! They stuffed their cheeks, reaching with clever hands into the feeder for more, depleting the seed supply.

Dad refilled the feeder right after lunch. Tam heard him telling someone about the squirrels and looked out to see Luke with Dad by the garage. She saw him rarely, so she seized the opportunity to thank him for bringing her home and to apologize for being a nuisance.

He virtually dwarfed her father. Before her courage could falter, she marched right up to Luke and spoke directly to the fourth button of his blue denim work shirt.

She met his eyes, which was difficult because his face

was so far up and because he looked through her. She also knew that he had seen her looking terrible too many times. One time was too many.

"I want to thank you..." she began, looking at the button.

Luke said, "Stewart would have come if he could. He won't be back until tomorrow. He must have told you."

He hadn't. Tam said nothing.

Luke said, "I know he'll feel terrible about being gone when you..."

"Don't remind me," Tam said. "I'm sorry to be such a n..."

"You're not. You have no reason to be embarrassed," said Luke. "Not with me, not ever. I thought you knew that." His eyes held hers, until she forced herself to look away.

"I'm not embarrassed," she lied.

"Yes, you are. Don't be."

She said nothing.

Luke said, "Don't worry about getting home tonight. Mack says to tell you to take today off instead of tomorrow."

"Mack said that?"

"On the phone this morning," said Luke, as if it were reasonable.

"Oh. Thank you," she said quietly.

"You're welcome." After a long silence, Luke said, "You need a baffle."

"Baffle?" echoed Tam, startled into looking up. Luke was talking to Dad, seeming to have forgotten her.

"Baffle?" she repeated.

Luke looked down at her. "For the squirrels," he explained, and, to Dad, "You need some obstacle that squirrels can't get past, like a barrier on the post. You can buy one but an old pie tin will do. Do you have one?"

For a moment she didn't realize the question was directed at her. Luke smiled. "Do you have a pie plate you don't need?" he repeated.

"Pie plate," said Tam. Luke nodded. She went to look and returned holding one out to him, "Will this do?"

"Thanks," said Luke, holding out his hand for the tin without glancing at her.

That man! She turned on her heel and huffed into the house. He was absolutely infuriating.

Except when she was in trouble, she thought, like the night before at the Food Mart. When she saw him there, she had known everything would be all right. Luke could handle it. She felt safe.

It must be his size, she thought, and his strength. If he weren't so enormous, he would be an ordinary person like everyone else. What else but his size made people put up with his directness and made them quote him incessantly?

They also know he means every word he says and every word is true.

Stop defending him, she told herself. *He's doing very well on his own. Better than I am.*

That man!

Dad came in pleased with himself and anxious for the squirrels to test the baffle. He sat by the window, but it was too dark to see the feeder, so he reluctantly turned on television for the first time that busy day.

Suddenly aware of the change in him, Tam saw his shoulders were straighter, his movements quicker and more certain, his general appearance more alert. It wasn't just an increased interest in feeding birds. It was an attitude of belonging to the active world.

Had Luke done this? Had those visits in the evenings while Tam was at work brought back her father's confidence? If so, she owed Luke thanks for this too.

She seldom saw him. He sort of came and went at the edges of her days, visiting with Dad when she was at work, working when she was at home, appearing only in disasters. Since the next week was peaceful, she didn't see him at all.

She went to work the next afternoon, Tuesday, embarrassed about being sent home like a child whose mother had sent big brother to collect her. Mack immediately let her know that Mr. Brill would never bother her again if Mack had anything to say about it. Then, satisfied that she had returned to normal, he put her up front on the cash register again.

Barb must have been satisfied with Tam's recovery. She resumed teasing where she had left off, joking about all the men coming to take Tam home. (Stewart and Luke, that is—Barb didn't mention Mr. Brill.)

"All kinds of handsome men are waiting in line to take me home," Tam told her.

"Of course," laughed Barb. "Don't they always? Which one can I have?"

"Take your choice," Tam told her. "If you take the one I want, I'll get another one."

"Which one do you want?" asked Barb.

"Be serious," said Tam, dismissing the joke, and the possibility, with a wave of her hand.

Catching Tam alone at break, Hope talked of church and Mrs. Warren's dinner before getting to what was on her mind. "You and Stewart kind of go together, huh?"

Tam said, "Not really. We haven't known each other very long. He just takes me home from work. What about you and Luke? You spent all afternoon together."

"Luke's nice," Hope said.

"Nice? That's all? After he followed you around all afternoon watching like diamonds would fall from your mouth? I bet he took you home." Tam was guessing correctly.

"Well, " Hope said, "Stewart offered, but Luke said he was going that direction anyway, so Luke drove me." Hope didn't look as pleased about that as Tam thought she would.

Tam said, "I think Luke's interested in you. He certainly hung on your every word. Every time you started to talk to Stewart, Luke was right there between you. If he drove you home, that proves it. He doesn't give up precious painting time for just anybody."

"He did for you," Hope said.

"That was an emergency. He'd do the same for a lost dog," Tam said.

"Maybe," Hope said, "but I think he likes you, not me. Don't you notice the way he watches every little thing you do?"

"He's an artist," Tam said. "Artists watch everybody and everything. Besides, if he likes me so much, why does he send Stewart to get me instead of coming himself? And why does he avoid me? I think he wants Stewart to keep me out of his hair."

"Maybe, but Luke says. . . ."

Tam groaned. "Oh, no. Not you too. Does everybody I know have to go around quoting that man?"

"I thought you'd like to know," Hope said. "Luke says

you're perfect for Stewart and Luke says if Stewart's got any sense at all he'll hang on to you."

"Luke said that?"

Hope nodded. "So I thought I would ask. . ."

"You know more about this than I do," said Tam. "Luke didn't tell me and I sincerely hope nobody tells Stewart. I don't like being pushed at him like a vitamin pill. Promise you won't say a word."

Hope promised. Quickly.

On the ride home, Tam tried to find out if Stewart knew Luke's opinion, but Stewart mostly seemed glad to be back and apologetic for not being there when Mr. Brill appeared. He'd gone to Ohio unexpectedly on family business, he said, and stayed through Monday to report to the Haberson's Company headquarters. He said they liked to know how things were progressing at the mall.

Stewart looked almost as angry about Mr. Brill as Luke had. "Call me immediately," he said, "if you ever need help."

Tam promised.

"Too bad about your dress," he said. "Mrs. Warren said you fixed it up better than new and she showed me the blouse you painted. Mrs. Warren told me you had talent, but I didn't realize you could do things like that. I'm impressed. You'll have to show me the dress."

Tam glowed under his praise. He liked her work and wanted to see the dress. If Tam were a large cat, she would have purred loudly with pleasure.

The talk turned to Mrs. Warren's dinner and Tam assured him, when he asked, that both Dad and Hope had enjoyed themselves.

"Nice girl, Hope," Stewart said.

"Yes," said Tam.

After breakfast the next morning, Tam took the dress next door so Mrs. Warren could show it to Stewart when he came home from work. Let Mrs. Warren show him, Tam thought, so I won't feel like a kindergarten child showing my finger-painting.

Mrs. Warren must have told him quite a lot. Stewart was all admiration and enthusiasm that night when he picked her up. He wanted to know where she got the pattern, how she knew what colors to use, the whole story.

"I just know," she said. "I've always liked designing things. Once I thought about studying interior decorating, but it didn't work out."

"Are you serious about wanting to design?"

"As serious as I can be, under the circumstances. Food Mart doesn't have much designing to do, besides displays and signs. Painting the dress was like breathing—that easy and much more fun. I really enjoyed it. I wish I could do more."

"Then why don't you?" he urged. "Get some silk blouses—three or four different ones. Paint them like you did Mrs. Warren's. You don't need many. Just a few samples. Then I'll take them around to two or three shops I know. I think when they see what you can do, they'll order some to sell."

"I can't," Tam said.

"Why not?"

"Nobody would buy them," she said, thinking it over.

"Leave that to me," said Stewart. "I'm a pretty good salesman when I've got something people want to buy."

Tam considered. "I can't. I don't have money to buy silk blouses. Mrs. Warren already had that white shirt and she gave me the dress. There's no way I can buy three or four silk blouses. It sounds terrific, but if I can't buy the blouses, I can't paint on them."

Stewart said, "I'll lend you the money."

"I couldn't take your money."

"Strictly business," he said. "Consider it a business investment. We'll draw it up nice and legal. You can pay me back when you sell your first order."

Tam was beginning to think this insane scheme might possibly work, but she was cautious. She said, "What happens if I don't sell any?"

"Then you'll pay me off in merchandise and I'll have Christmas presents for four lucky ladies," he said, laughing. "Don't worry about it. They will sell. Your biggest problem will be producing them fast enough to fill the orders. I'll take them around to a couple of friends of mine in the business, and you'll have more orders than you know what to do with. Luke says. . ."

Not Luke again, Tam thought, but she didn't say it. She said, "You and Luke have already talked this over?"

"It was his idea," Stewart said. "Mrs. Warren thought it was a good idea, too. She says she'll go with you to buy the blouses, if you want her to. Your dad should be able to handle the bookkeeping. Luke says your dad knows all about that sort of thing. Mrs. Warren will help you shop, your dad can keep the books, and I'll do the selling. All you have to do is create beautiful clothes. Yes?"

"I don't know," Tam said slowly.

"Luke says he's never seen anything like them. He says you can't miss."

"All right. I'll do it," she decided, right there in the driveway, and suddenly she was determined to make it

work. *Crazy. Impossible,* **she thought.** *I might regret it, but I'll do it. We'll do it.*

eight

The business of painting silk blouses moved rapidly. They all caught the success bug.

Stewart sent them to a wholesale contact of his in Indianapolis, because they needed to get many of the same kind of blouse and only a wholesaler or manufacturer could offer that at reasonable cost.

Mrs. Warren consulted Tam about color and style, then took Tam's opinion about color and chose the style herself.

"We carry three qualities," said the short, round-faced wholesaler, "and seconds. If you want seconds, I'll make you a special price."

"How much?" asked Tam.

"No, thank you," said Mrs. Warren.

"But I might make a mistake. I can't paint on something perfect," argued Tam.

Mrs. Warren said, "Of course you can, dear," and bought six beautiful silk blouses in five luscious pastels and one white. "If you want to do business with fine shops, you have to provide fine merchandise. Our clientele will be expecting luxury. Luke says. . ."

"Never mind."

Mrs. Warren brought paints and brushes over, explaining, "Luke says you should use acrylic paint, not oil, because acrylic dries faster and is more flexible on fabric. He says you can manage it if you work fast. He says he isn't

118

going to use these and you might like to have them."

"Luke says. Luke says," muttered Tam under her breath.

"What, dear?"

Tam said, "Please tell Luke I said thank you." She knew better than to argue. She also had sense enough to do it his way.

Soon she was painting expertly, creating beautiful designs, and humming as she worked. *I never had so much fun,* she thought. *I told Stewart painting those clothes was like breathing, but it's better.*

She studied each blouse, then mixed the colors she felt, put a brush to them, and out came the flowers, flowing through her fingers like water through a pipe. Each blouse was a little different, but they all bore the distinct mark of her hand, identifiable immediately as hers.

In a week they were finished and hanging in the cleared hall closet. They looked so pretty there that Tam couldn't shut the closet door on the little cluster of flowers.

Stewart looked them over and nodded enthusiastically. "You need a name for this line," he said, "a label. Something like 'Fashions by Tam.'"

"Or 'Tamara's Silks'," suggested Mrs. Warren.

"It sounds like race horses," said Stewart. How about 'Floating Flowers'?"

"Water ballet," objected Mrs. Warren.

Dad said, on paper, that the poet Robert Frost had referred to butterflies as "flowers that fly." So how about "Tamara's butterflies"? or just "Butterflies"?

"'Butterflies?' Perfect!" pronounced Mrs. Warren.

"I like it," said Stewart.

"Me too," echoed Tam. "I didn't know you read Robert Frost, Dad."

"No," said Dad and wrote, "Luke."

"Of course. I should have known," said Tam.

Tam painted labels on silk ribbon and Mrs. Warren sewed them in. They could order professional labels later.

Dad was in his element, delighted to prove himself valuable. Using his bookkeeping, he established a tentative wholesale price, which he doubled to a suggested retail price.

Tam gasped at the retail price. "I could buy a whole outfit for that."

"Not a designer original," Mrs. Warren said. "I think it's quite reasonable."

"We'll know soon enough when I take these samples around to a few buyers," said Stewart, taking her Butterflies, each meticulously ironed and encased in its own cleaner's bag from Mrs. Warren's collection. "Don't worry," he said, several times. "And don't ask. I'll let you know when I have orders. Don't worry."

That week Barb caught Tam humming at work, several times. "You're in love," Barb said.

"I am," Tam agreed. "I'm in love with painting silk blouses."

Barb shook her head. "You're in love with Stewart."

Tam laughed at that. "Be serious, Barb. Stewart's a friend."

"Friend!" Barb snorted. "Stewart's not a friend. He's a dream. Listen to Barbara. Grab him before some other girl gets him."

"That's a little cold-blooded," Tam said.

Barb said, "Not if he loves you."

"He doesn't," Tam said.

"Of course he does. And you love him. Look at you.

You're a different person. I tell you that man is good for you."

She had a point. Tam was happier. Painting blouses was a joy. Dad was alert and more confident. Tam felt better and she knew she looked better.

Maybe Barb is right, Tam reflected. Maybe I'm in love and don't know it.

Stewart certainly had all the right ingredients for a dream come true. Did he love her? That didn't seem likely. But he did appear every night and always seemed glad to be with her. Perhaps he did love her, a little.

"I don't know, Barb," Tam said. "I thought if you were in love you'd know it. Bells ring or something."

"Don't believe that stuff," Barb said. "That's only in books."

Tam said, "I was in love once. In high school. I knew that time, no question. Fireworks went off every time we got near each other."

"You were a kid. Now you're a grown-up," Barb said. "It's different."

"I don't know," Tam said. To Barb she might be a different person, but parts of her were unchanged.

One part of her was caution, she thought. She didn't jump into things. The last thing she had jumped into was Mr. Brill's car, and that had been a mistake. She wouldn't have jumped into the blouse business, but she was pushed. Besides, she had already tried painting and knew she could do it.

Another part of her was stubbornness that made her keep going when anyone else would say she had already been beaten.

Practicality was another part, useful when her pride

wouldn't let her quit.

The odd part, the part that didn't belong with the rest, the part Barb refused to recognize, was romance. Barb said to forget romance, but she didn't want to. She needed to believe that love is possible—if not for her, then for other people.

Barb would say that was dumb, that Tam should grab what she could, but Barb's love had gone bitter. If Tam couldn't find real love for herself, she was sure she would know it. She told Barb that then, and the next night, and the night after that.

Barb kept telling Tam how handsome and successful Stewart was, how smooth his manners were, how good they looked together. She said Tam would be a fine wife for a rising executive.

That last point was debatable, Tam thought. Stewart was too classy for her, too sophisticated. Still, with more time and more money she might look classy too.

Maybe not, she thought. *I'd spend that time and money doing something I really want to do. Other girls can paint their toenails and embroider rosebuds on their underwear. If I had the time and money, I'd study art. I'd paint or design or. . .*

Hope never stayed around to listen when Barb started teasing Tam. To Tam it seemed reasonable that Hope wanted to avoid such scenes. Some other things seemed less reasonable.

For example, some nights Stewart would ask Hope if he and Tam could drop her off on the way home, although Hope lived in the opposite direction.

Irrelevant. Stewart was generous with his car.

Hope always said she'd rather walk, that she needed the

exercise. she'd walk past the car and out of the lot, Stewart watching her go. Something about this felt wrong, but Tam couldn't put her finger on it, so she tried to shrug it off.

Sunday morning Mrs. Warren assumed Dad and Tam would go to church with them. Dad didn't put up a fuss. He preened himself in the blue blazer and Tam wafted around in her designer silk dress. . . an original Butterfly. *The* original Butterfly.

At church, Mrs. Warren left them to go down to her primary class, and they went upstairs to join Hope in Adult Bible Study Class. Dad liked to sit on the aisle, any aisle, so Tam hung back to sit with him. Luke shuffled in first, next to Hope, followed by Stewart and Tam, and then Dad. It crossed Tam's mind that Luke had arranged again to keep Hope to himself and away from Stewart. Possible? Definitely!

Tam hadn't attended Sunday school in years, since youth group had met in this room on Sunday nights before adjourning to the basement for games and ham salad sandwiches over those years, and an unknown number of chocolate cupcakes.

This adult class was following Paul's journeys, which Tam found fascinating. Dad seemed interested too. Perhaps he would come again.

After class they meandered into the sanctuary, stopping every few feet to talk to acquaintants. Dad and Mrs. Warren sat in back and Hope led the rest to the front. This time Tam watched and, sure enough, Luke arranged things so they sat in the same order until Hope traded Luke places to sit by Tam. Tam wondered if Hope realized how efficiently Luke was keeping her to himself.

Let him sit by her, Tam thought wryly. Let him see what good it does him. When church starts, she won't even know he's there.

At the Call to Worship, Tam saw that Hope had begun to close out distractions. A penny hit the floor nearby and a fan buzzed faintly, but Hope was oblivious to those noises.

Stewart seemed as absorbed as Hope. Was Luke? Tam leaned a bit forward and stretched to see his face, half expecting to meet his eyes. They were closed. His face was softer than usual, more peaceful. Seeing him this way, Tam realized how stern and intense he often was.

One of Tam's old friends with whom she had lost touch, Marg, sang a solo, like she often had when they were in school together. Her voice was rich and full, improved with time, and as Tam listened, time ran backward. Marg and Tam were kids again, with Ben in the pew watching Marg, and Robert next to Tam. Marg poured her feelings into the air. The music stopped in the hushed sanctuary and a man across the aisle breathed a soft amen. Tam turned to share with Robert. But it wasn't Robert. It was Stewart, and she covered her face with her hands.

If I had known, she thought, *I would not have come.*

Squaring her shoulders, she pulled her hands down, away from her face and folded them tightly in her lap. She hoped Stewart hadn't noticed.

She would be more wary. She would protect herself by keeping joy at a distance so joy would not open the gates to old sorrow. Tougher is better. *Use your mind,* she said to herself. *Keep your heart out of this. Concentrate.*

She concentrated on the Road to Emmaus in the stained glass window, glowing in the sunlight above Luke's head and lost herself in the vibrant colors again.

They were walking, she and another traveler, and a Stranger joined them. They told Him about Jesus. He told them more than they knew about God, more than the rabbis in the temple knew. Tam wondered at His wisdom, but she did not guess who He was.

That's where her imagination always ended. She never got to the village, never reached the part where her eyes were opened and she suddenly knew Him. Would she have recognized Him, if she had been on that ordinary dusty road from one town to the next?

People's heads were bowed and she realized that Mr. Moore was closing his sermon with prayer. Another Sunday, she thought, without finding the key to understanding.

Another hymn and the benediction, and they filed out. In the aisle and at the door, on the outside steps and on the sidewalk in front of the church, people greeted each other and chatted. Tam wanted out. She needed time to think.

Dad and Mrs. Warren met friends. Hope dashed away to catch a girl she knew from college. Stewart stood involved in conversation about building supplies with Ben, Marg's husband.

Tam found a place apart from smiles and handshakes, under the little maple between the sidewalk and the curb. She waited there silently.

"You've had a long morning." Luke's deep voice startled her. She hadn't seen him approach.

"What?" she said.

"I was saying that you've had a long morning. A difficult morning."

Tam studied her shoes. "Yes," she murmured. "I was thinking of other things."

"Like the stained glass window?" he asked.

Tam had thought no one saw.

"And the solo?" he went on.

Tam abruptly turned her back to him and his words. She shut him out to protect herself. Luke had a way of going directly to her hidden hurts and uncovering them. He knew too much.

"Tell me," he ordered, gently.

She shook her head, standing with her back to him until Stewart returned with Hope. She wanted to walk home alone. Luke was right; she'd had a long morning.

That was the trouble with Luke, she decided. He was always right. He'd be easier to like if he weren't so nosy, so perceptive.

Hope walked next to Tam, keeping the silence.

Hope? Was Hope going to Mrs. Warren's again? Luke was determined to be with her!

Fine, thought Tam. *Let Hope spend the afternoon being the object of Luke's attention. She can have my share. I just want to go home.*

"Only a light lunch," Mrs. Warren was saying. "I know you like to eat conservatively."

"No," smiled Dad, accepting for himself and Tam. He did things like that, forgot she was a grown-up person who might have ideas of her own, instead of just a daughter.

"Okay, Tam?" asked Mrs. Warren.

Tam smiled and nodded. What else could she do?

Mrs. Warren's light buffet lunch was light only in color: pale pink cold cuts, salads of pastel greens and yellows, pink gelatin, beige breads, and homemade bread-and-butter pickles in a color-coordinated pale grayed-green dish. It looked cool and inviting. If Tam could have eaten alone, if she were hungry, she would have enjoyed it.

She wasn't hungry but couldn't say so. Instead she chose foods which took lots of plate space, but little stomach space.

One thin slice of ham covered half her plate. If she did it right, using her fork to cut it into meticulously measured little bites, she could make a slice of ham last for at least ten minutes, maybe more. Carrot sticks and celery stuffed with cream cheese were good time wasters and, artistically arranged on her plate, they took up lots of space. The rest of the plate was covered by lettuce, a wonderful space waster.

Selecting took a long time. That was the point. Time spent selecting was time she didn't have to spend sitting, arranging and rearranging carrot sticks. It was also easier to avoid talking to people at the buffet table than at her place. Then she sat.

Suddenly Stewart said, "What about you, Tam?'

Everybody waited for her answer, but she didn't know the question. She blinked.

"Of course she does," said Mrs. Warren.

Tam nodded. It must be the right answer. Conversation resumed and Tam returned to her lettuce.

Of course I do what? She wished she had been listening. She peeked at her watch. One thirty. At two she could excuse herself to go get ready for work. She could go now. She rose to carry her plate into the kitchen.

Mrs. Warren took it. "You go on upstairs, dear. "I'll take care of the dishes."

"I have to go to work," Tam said vaguely.

"I know. You'd better look right away if you want to see them, and I know you do. Luke?" Mrs. Warren handed

Tam over to Luke, who said, "Stewart?" and handed Tam over to Stewart. She felt like one of the plates.

Mrs. Warren said, "Come on, Hope, if you want to see Luke's paintings," and Hope rose also.

Stewart followed Tam to the foot of the attic steps, where they filed behind Luke up to the studio.

Ironic, Tam thought. *If they had asked me yesterday, I'd have jumped at the chance to see his paintings. I'd like to know if he's any good and what kinds of subjects attract this man who sees through people and knows too much.*

Today though, she didn't want to be within fifty feet of Luke. Bad enough to have him watching her in church and prying into her thoughts afterward without having to look at his pictures and make polite compliments. *Suppose he is awful,* she thought. *What will I say?*

She checked her watch again.

Luke opened the attic door and flipped the light switch. He waited there to catch their initial reactions. Tam knew that trick. She'd done it herself to see people's true feelings in that split second before they drop polite masks over their faces. He wouldn't catch her off guard. Not again.

But he did.

The power of his work sprang out at her as she came through the door. Canvas after canvas spoke of passion and pain as clearly as if they had shouted. More clearly. They lined the walls and leaned in groups against the upright beams—dozens of them, dozens of shouts of pain and cries of sorrow, condensed emotion, solid, almost tangible.

Tam raised her hand to ward it off. Her eyes stung with it and her throat ached. It pulled her closer, to stand before one after another of the paintings. Absorbed, she forgot

Luke and Stewart and Hope. She moved slowly down the rows, studying each piece.

As she moved, she felt the sorrow in the paintings gradually give way to anger. An undercurrent in some of the paintings, anger surged to dominance in others. A few were pure rage made graphic in brush strokes. These frightened her. She backed away.

Luke's hand on her arm stopped her before she backed into an easel. His eyes were anxious. She searched them for the fury she saw in his work, but there was none. What she saw there was something she couldn't read. Sorrow? Not quite. What?

Luke led her to the other side of the attic where more canvasses crowded floor and walls. These were different. By another artist, she guessed at first, until closer inspection showed the swift power of Luke's hand. Here was no anger. Sorrow still, and pain, but the shout had become only a murmur. Here was calm.

Smoother brush strokes, gentler shapes, and a softer palette with subtler transitions between colors made peace with the power behind the hand. There were faces here, as there were on the other side of the attic, but these were not twisted. There were landscapes here, with trees and streams instead of the torn and blackened ruins in the other pictures. It was relief from the anger and pain. Here was peace and comfort, and she stood before them, opening her heart to them, feeling them spread comfort on her own spirit.

"Tam?" Mrs. Warren called from the bottom of the stairs. "Tam, you have to go. It's after two."

Already? She had just come up the stairs. "Coming," Tam called.

She looked around for Stewart and Hope, but they had gone. She'd been so engrossed in Luke's work that she was unaware of anything else.

And she hadn't seen all the paintings. Under the dormer window was another stack. She couldn't resist a fast look before she left. She put her hand on the corner of the first one in the stack to turn it so she could see it.

"No!" barked Luke.

Tam froze, her hand still on the canvas.

"No," he said, in apologetic gentleness, "Not those."

She took her hand away. "Sorry," she said.

"No, don't be."

"They're wonderful. Thank you." She reached out to touch the hand that created those paintings. He closed her small hand in his two large ones.

"Tam," called Mrs. Warren again.

He opened his hands as if releasing a butterfly and Tam pulled her hand away, unable to break the gaze that bound her to him. Then she shut her eyes and turned abruptly, hurrying down the stairs and out, calling her thanks to Mrs. Warren as she ran.

Stewart was waiting with the engine running when she had rushed into work clothes and out to the car. She hopped in and slid low in the seat to catch her breath. Luke's paintings had taken her by surprise and she was profoundly moved by the depth of them.

Stewart said, "Luke's a pretty good artist."

She said, "He's wonderful."

Stewart laughed. "I told you he was," he said. "Why are you surprised?"

"I guess I didn't expect quite that much. I had no idea he felt so much sorrow and anger."

Stewart said, "It's the war, partly, I guess. None of us are the same after we see buddies blown to bits and innocent people destroyed. He never talks about it, but I know he hasn't forgotten. And of course, his wife is part of it."

"His wife?" Something lurched in Tam's chest. She swallowed and said, "I didn't know he was married."

"No, you wouldn't," Stewart said. "He never mentions her. She died in a car accident while he was overseas. By the time the news reached him, she'd been dead and buried more than a week. He never shed a tear, not then. Just went out and killed as many soldiers as he could for the next three days. Dived into them like he didn't care if he lived or died. That's how we got trapped and knocked out of action for a while.

"He carried me out of there. I never could have made it if he hadn't. By the time they decided we were well enough to send back to the front lines, the fighting had stopped and they didn't need us anymore."

"So you came home together," Tam prompted.

"Yes."

"What about his family?" Tam asked.

"Dead."

"Oh."

They rode in silence for a while, each deep in private thoughts. Tam's went back to the paintings. She understood now. The anger must have come before the sorrow, not the other way, as she had first thought. She was misled by the order in which she'd seen them. The peaceful ones must have been painted first, before the troubles, although the technique in those was so far advanced from the others and the touch so much surer that Tam had felt certain they were painted afterward.

Stewart said, "The angry paintings, then the sad ones, were done in the hospital and when he came home to his wife's grave. The other ones, the quiet ones, were painted after he met Jesus."

After he met Jesus. Did Jesus do that—change ferocious violence and unbearable pain to peace? He must have. Tam had seen the evidence. All her life she had heard of the power of God to change men's lives, but this was the first time she had actually seen it for herself.

Luke's paintings told their story. The fury gave way to grief and then to misery. She had seen the transitions. The other paintings were entirely different, with no transition. Changed totally.

Traces of sorrow remained. She'd seen that. But the sorrow was no longer dominant. It was present, but it was subdued. Not tightly controlled like the tears of a man refusing to cry. Eased. Acknowledged and eased.

"Is that what Luke says? That it changed after he met Jesus?" she asked.

Stewart nodded. "That's what Luke says."

nine

Barb was wild that night, heckling co-workers and customers alike. Tam recognized this mood and knew Barb
was working off tension.

"What's wrong?" asked Tam.

"Nothing," Barb snapped.

"None of your business," she said when Tam asked
again.

"Nothing I can't handle," she said the third time, but this
time she answered more gently. Tam asked again.

"My daughter," Barb said. "Sara wouldn't eat supper
and cried when I left for work. That's not like her." Barb's
sister thought it was just a mood, but Barb didn't agree and
said she'd feel better if she were home, but she couldn't
afford to lose the work hours.

"Your sister will know what to do," Tam said. "Phone
home at the break. If you want to go home then, go. It's
a slow night. Vickie and I can manage."

Barb was calmer after that, but tighter. She had started
out laughing, letting off steam in play. Now her play got
rougher. If Hope had been there, Hope would have been
miserable.

At break, Barb learned Sara had a fever, but her sister said
children often have light fevers that disappear as mysteri-
ously as they begin. If the fever went up, she'd call the
doctor. Barb might as well stay at work.

Barb stopped playing.

At 10:58 Barb left the register for the back room, pulling off her smock as she went through beauty and hygiene. Going to punch out, Tam met Barb hurrying to the front door.

"Let us take you home," Tam offered. "Stewart won't mind. Wait for me out front. I'll hurry." Without waiting for an answer, Tam dashed to punch out.

On her way up front, Tam saw Barbara and Mack near the office arguing angrily. Mack was pulling at Barb's smock, trying to snatch it from her hands. Barb clutched it tightly, pulling toward the exit. She jerked the smock. Tam heard the rip of fabric and the thunk of plastic hitting the floor. A bottle of aspirin lay there between them. Mack bent down and picked it up. He held it close to Barbara's face and leaned his own face closer.

His voice was angry, but too low for Tam to understand the words. She could guess. Barb had hidden the aspirin in the pocket of the smock, like the gum, and Mack had caught her, tonight of all nights.

Barb argued, red-faced, but Mack turned his back and left her standing with the torn smock dangling from her fingers. She turned abruptly, stamped to the door, and was outside before Tam caught her.

"What happened?" Tam asked.

Barb jerked out of Tam's grasp. "He fired me."

"Are you sure?" Tam said. "Maybe he's just mad."

Barb said, "I'm sure. He doesn't want me back, not even to pick up my pay. Would you. . ."

"Sure. I'll pick it up and bring it to you," said Tam, "but did you apologize? Did you tell him you're upset about your daughter? Did you offer to pay for the aspirin? Did you. . ."

Tam knew by the set of Barb's jaw that arguing was useless. Barb wanted to go home.

In Stewart's car Barb bumped along in the cramped back seat in tight-lipped silence. Her face was ashen. She did not cry.

At her apartment she squeezed out before Tam could lean the seat forward. "Thanks," she said, rushing off.

"I'll call you," Tam shouted after her.

Barb waved her hand to signify that she had heard, and disappeared into the dark building.

"Thanks for taking her home," Tam said to Stewart, and explained what had happened. Together they sorted through the few possibilities, trying to find a way to help. Tam could try to get Mack to let her come back. Stewart could see if he could find her a job. They'd offer to help, especially if Sara was worse in the morning.

That's all they could think of, except, Stewart said, to pray. Sitting in the driveway, Stewart held Tam's hand and they bowed their heads together asking God's help for Barbara and her daughter.

Tam wondered what good her little prayer would do, since she was not on close terms with God. But Stewart was. God would listen to him, she thought, and she felt better.

"Thanks for listening," she said. She gave his hand a little squeeze and let go. "And thanks for caring about Barbara. You're a good friend.

Stewart looked at Tam oddly and took her hand again. "Is that what I am? A good friend? I thought I was more than that."

She stared at him, slowly comprehending.

He saw her confusion and chuckled.

"Don't laugh at me," she said.

"I can't help it," he said. "You're funny. You really never believed I might be interested in you, did you? I drive you home every night and spend my free time helping you get started in business so you can do something you enjoy for a change. I sit next to you in church and walk you home and you think I am nothing more than a friend. Do you think I do this for every pretty girl I meet?"

Tam said nothing, confused.

Stewart went on, "You *do*, don't you! Only, you don't think you're pretty. Luke said that but I didn't believe it. I've seen so many girls who pretended they were modest that I didn't recognize the real thing when I saw it. You don't realize how attractive you are." With his free hand he traced the side of her cheek. "For your information, Miss Tamara, you're a very attractive young lady and I have been more than interested in you for a long time. Come here, pretty girl."

He leaned closer. His lips brushed her forehead and then, tilting her face up to meet his, he kissed her lightly on the lips. He leaned back a little to study her face. Then he opened the door and came around the car to let her out.

Somehow she got into the house without letting him see her face again. Before she let him see her turmoil, she had to understand it herself. She shut the door tightly behind her and leaned on it, letting out a long, slow breath.

She had never imagined. Barb had been teasing her for weeks and she never seriously thought it was possible that Barb could be right. It still didn't make sense. Why would Stewart—polished, gorgeous, successful Stewart—be attracted to Tam?

A thousand girls would jump at the chance to go out with him. Look at the way they all reacted when they met him. She herself had stammered and stumbled like a child. Barbara and Vickie had stopped in their tracks. Even Hope, with her silky hair and college freshness, had been fascinated. The man had everything.

Tam had nothing to offer him. She took quick inventory: Grace? Wit? Style? *Don't be silly,* she said to herself. Education? Social connection? Zero. Personality? She wasn't sure she still had one. Good looks? Definitely not, no matter what he said.

How about modesty? *No,* she thought, *just honesty.*

On the other hand, she thought, *I'm not a total waste of protoplasm. I'm a hard worker. I have some art talent. I can make a small income go a long way. And I don't cry easily, although sometimes I'm not as tough as I'd like to believe.*

I like dogs and children. And birds. What more could a handsome man like Stewart want?

Be serious.

Tam had tea with Dad and told him about Barb and tucked him in for the night. He was in a strange mood, she thought—very mysterious. He seemed to know something she didn't and he wasn't telling. She asked if anything was wrong, but he passed it off with a funny grin. She shrugged and let it go. If it was important, it would come out soon. For a man with speech problems, he had a hard time keeping secrets. Besides, she had her own secrets.

When he was in bed, she returned for another cup of tea, and turning the ceiling light out, sat in the dim kitchen, listening to the refrigerator hum and letting her tangled feelings unravel.

Stewart seemed sincere when he said she was pretty, but she knew she wasn't. Perhaps pretty to him meant something other than it meant to Tam. Perhaps to him all girls were pretty.

Luke had said she didn't think she was pretty and he was right. He knew because he saw her the way she saw herself. He would. He had an artist's eye. He wouldn't miss the sprinkling of gray in her dark hair nor the purple ink stains on her hands. He wouldn't dismiss her thinness as ethereal nor her short stature as cute. He would register the worn sneakers and the dismal cottons she wore day after day, except on Sundays, when she blossomed in silk.

Still, Stewart said she was pretty, and he'd kissed her. Not a passionate embrace, it's true, but a kiss. Two.

What would Luke say about that?

Tam knew what Barbara would say. She'd already heard it.

And what did Tam say? That sitting in the open car with a picture-book hero holding her hand and kissing her lightly on the forehead and lips was romantic. She'd do it again, if she could. She would definitely do it again.

Why not?

If Stewart wanted to kiss her and drive her around, who was she to question it? Enjoy it, she told herself. Don't question a gift like this. Accept it.

When she went to bed, she didn't look to see if the light was on in the attic next door. She almost did, out of habit, but she caught herself. She didn't want to think about Luke up there anymore. She wanted to think about Stewart and the kiss in the car.

She closed her eyes and tried to feel the kiss again.

Nothing. She tried again, this time going back to the prayer and reliving the conversation, working up to the kiss.

No use. Images of Luke's canvasses crowded into her mind. She shut her eyes tighter to erase them. Behind her lids, Luke's rage and grief cried out in passionate colors. Very well then, if she could not shut out his paintings, she would select a particular one to remember. A peaceful one.

In her mind she ranged through the collection of peaceful canvasses, settling on one that had particularly attracted her—a landscape, with a country road next to a meandering stream. The scene was familiar. Oh, of course. It was like the stained glass window in church—the Road to Emmaus.

The road beckoned and she wandered down it. A Stranger met her and walked with her and they talked. She didn't recognize Him, even in the dream.

Monday she spent the morning catching up on the work she hadn't done the week before. It busied her and that was good, because if she stopped to think, she might have frightened herself out of her resolve to enjoy Stewart's company. This was one of the days he planned to contact a potential buyer for her Butterflies. Between hoping for a sale and trying not to think about Stewart, she was torn in two directions. She needed to keep busy.

She called Barb, who was feeling both better and worse. Sara had chicken pox, which was unpleasant but not terrible. The doctor said it was good thing she hadn't given Sara aspirin, since that might have caused serious complications.

Tam didn't point out that of all nights for her to be caught stealing, that was the right night because it kept her from accidentally harming Sara. She did ask if Barb had reconsidered apologizing.

She had. She had telephoned but Mack wouldn't listen. Tam had no more ideas. All she could give was sympathy and encouragement. Tomorrow she'd do what Mrs. Warren would have done—take Barb a casserole. It couldn't hurt.

Stewart asked about Barb when he picked Tam up from work. He also wanted to know if Tam would enjoy dinner in a restaurant with him at, say, seven the next evening. Tam would, but checked with Dad to see if he objected to eating alone. He didn't seem pleased, but he didn't object.

When Stewart came for her, Dad was waiting in the kitchen for Luke, who had promised him a game of chess. Dad hardly looked up as they left, not even to tell them to have a good time.

They went to Chez Raoul, the poshest place within twenty miles. Stewart said it was the only place stylish enough for Tam's silk dress. It was so stylish that Tam couldn't read the menu. It was in French, six pages of it. Tam didn't recognize, and couldn't find, chicken. She also couldn't order by picking the cheapest thing on the menu because her copy had no prices. She let Stewart order.

"Have you been here before?" he asked, when he and the waiter had decided what Tam would eat.

"Not since it was Napoli's Pizza Palace," she said. "It looks different with tablecloths."

Napoli wouldn't have recognized the old place. Chez Raoul was dark, lit by candles. As her eyes adjusted to the dimness, she squinted at the pictures on the walls. She couldn't see them. From the darkest corner, behind what seemed to be an enormous blue chicken, came piano music. The player must be blind, she thought. Who else would be able to find the keys?

"What do you think of the place?" Stewart asked.

"Very romantic," she said, twisting her napkin.

"That's the idea." He pried one of her hands away from the napkin and spread the hand, palm down, on the corner of the table. In the darkness the purple ink on her fingers was barely visible. He traced each finger with his own, slowly, and then covered her hand with his hand. She watched.

When dinner arrived, she slid her hand off the table and picked up her fork. In the dark, she could distinguish lighter and darker lumps, largish ones, in some kind of sauce.

"What is it?" she asked.

"Poulet en Cocotte a la Paysanne," said Stewart.

She stirred it about, cautiously, and took a very tiny taste, then a bigger taste. "Mmmm," she said. "Delicious. I'm so glad you did the ordering. I'd probably have gotten something ordinary, like chicken."

"It *is* chicken. Poulet is French for chicken.

"Oh. It's delicious."

They ate slowly. Stewart talked of many things: his family in Ohio, the job, his plans, many things. She listened, thinking he was easy to listen to.

They selected desserts from the dessert cart—a napoleon for Tam, because she especially like them, and a strawberry tart for Stewart. Then she had tea; he had coffee. They dawdled over the drinks, making playful conversation. She forgot her nerves and had a wonderful time. Robert had never taken her to a place like this.

We were too young then to appreciate it, she thought. *Now I am exactly the right age for Chez Raoul.*

She was exactly the right age to be kissed in the moonlight too. When he leaned toward her and slid his arm around her shoulders she was nervous, but she lifted her lips to meet his in a long, lingering gentle kiss. And another. She sighed and leaned against his shoulder, filling her nose with the scent of his shaving lotion.

"Thank you," she whispered. "It was wonderful."

"Yes, it was," he whispered, lowering his lips for another kiss.

"The dinner, I mean," she said, pulling back.

"That too," he said, and kissed her again.

He would have kissed her at the door too if she'd stood still long enough, or if Dad hadn't been sitting at the kitchen table waiting, with all the lights on, including the one over the door. Instead she said a quick good night and watched him go off to his own door.

At that moment she thought she saw a shadow move at the attic window, just flicker across it and vanish. She peered more closely, but saw nothing in the attic light.

Did she have a nice time, Dad asked her, and where's the tea? She might have been coming home from work, no more, instead of returning from the first real date she'd had in years. Here she was with news to share, and no listener. *Wait,* she thought. *Just wait until he wants to show me some new bird!*

In the morning Dad was indifferent to her adventure and Mrs. Warren was entirely absent. The excitement cooled and she was left with doubts to mull over alone.

Halfway to work she remembered the casserole she had meant to make for Barbara and was immediately stricken with remorse. She'd better phone at break.

Hope worked Wednesday, which was unusual. Mack was filling in Barb's hours with part-timers. Hope was glad to have the extra time so when Mack called her she jumped at the chance for more pay. College is expensive.

"I wish I didn't feel like I was taking food from Barbara's mouth," Hope said, punching in.

"You are," said Vickie, who was not in a forgiving mood. "You got her fired. If you hadn't told Mack on her, she'd be at that register tonight, instead of you."

Hope's mouth dropped open. "I didn't. I wouldn't do that."

"Not much you wouldn't." said Vickie.

Hope looked for help to Tam, who shook her head slightly to indicate the futility of arguing. It would only make things worse.

The three worked next to each other in strained silence for almost an hour before Hope dropped a closed sign onto her conveyor counter. She said, "That's all. I can't stand it anymore."

"What are you going to do?" asked Vickie.

"Quit," said Hope. "Then Mack will have to call Barbara back."

"Good idea," said Vickie.

Tam said, "Don't do it. It won't work. He'll hire somebody new and you'll be out of a job."

"Good," said Vickie.

"I have to do something," Hope said.

"I'll talk to Mack," said Tam. "Maybe he'll change his mind." She didn't intend to say that. The words flew out of her mouth before her brain could stop them. She had no idea how to get Mack to listen, but she had said too much to back out.

Hope went with her to the office, and then Vickie dropped a closed sign on her aisle and followed.

The first thing Mack said when he saw all three at the office was, "No registers are open."

"We'll open as soon as you talk with us," Tam said.

He said, "If it's about Barbara, I don't want to hear it. You three knew she was stealing and covered up for her. Now you come around wanting favors. Forget it."

"We do want a favor," Tam said. "We want you to give her another chance."

Mack snorted. "Why? So she can steal more? That stuff costs money. Little by little she costs this store a fortune."

"How much?" asked Tam.

"Huh? Oh, I don't know exactly. I'd have to figure it out. It's not just one bottle of aspirin, you know." Mack's crossed arms and stubborn jaw indicated little mercy.

"I know. You figure it out and tell me how much. I'll pay for it," Tam said, setting her jaw as stubbornly as Mack's.

"You can't," said Hope.

"I will. Mack, you figure it out and take it out of my pay every week, ten dollars, until it's all paid. How's that?" Tam folded her arms to match Mack's folded arms.

"It's no good," said Mack. "She'll run you into the poor house."

"Not if you tell her I have to pay for whatever she takes," Tam argued. "She knows I can't afford it."

Mack thought it over. "It might work at that. Barb's a good checker and it's worth a try. I'll tell you what. We'll try it for a month and see how it goes. If she doesn't rack up more debt, she can stay. I hate to do this to you though,

Tam."

"You're not. It's my own choice." Tam was firm in that.

"I hope she appreciates it," he said.

Tam smiled and put her hand out to shake on the deal. Barb wouldn't have to appreciate it to make Tam happy. All she had to do was get her job back and hang onto it. That was worth ten dollars a week to Tam.

Hope offered to help pay, but Tam didn't want her to. Tam had made the deal, so she intended to be the one to stick to it.

"You were terrific," said Hope, out of Mack's hearing.

Tam said, "Not really. I didn't know I was going to say that."

Vickie turned on Hope with scathing sarcasm. "You weren't so terrific, Hope. If you and your God are as close as you claim, why didn't you ask Him to do something about Barb's job?'

Hope smiled. "I did."

"So?" said Vickie.

"So He sent Tam," she said, and smiled at Tam's blank look.

Crazy, Tam thought. *I went to the office because I decided to, not because I was sent. But where did I get the words that made Mack take Barb back? Not from me. I was as surprised to hear it as anybody. Could Hope be right?*

Vickie had the last word. She said, "Barb's not going to like this." Tam hoped she was wrong.

She was. The next night Barb was early. She was huffy and stand-offish, letting on that she was doing Mack a favor by coming back, but they all knew she was glad to be there. Mack ignored her and after a while she stopped trying to cover her feelings.

At break Barb wanted to thank Tam, saying, "I never thought a friend would do that for me. I'll pay back every penny. Honest."

Tam laughed, "You'd better. I'm only doing this because I can't work here without you to pester me."

Barb put out her hand to Hope in apology. She was sorry, she said, about the way she had acted in the past. She had accused Hope of getting her fired, but now she knew that wasn't true and wanted to apologize. "Friends?" she asked.

"Friends," said Hope.

"I might even go to that church of yours some time," Barb ventured, and laughed in embarrassment, then scooted out the door before she exposed more softness.

"Look what you did," said Hope to Tam.

"I can't claim credit for that. I just did what came to mind," Tam said. "Ten dollars isn't such a big deal, if you think about it."

"If you can see that, you should be able to understand why God gave His Son for us," Hope said. "He's the best Friend we have."

"Then why don't I feel what you feel in church?" Tam asked. "You get more out of it than I do. You seem to soak that stuff up. My mind wanders. I think about all kinds of things. I hear the songs and the prayers, but they're not inside me. Not the way they are with you."

"That's because Jesus isn't in your heart yet. Once you let Him in, your whole life is different."

Tam said, "I don't think I really know Him. I can't seem to find Him."

Hope said, "Just ask. That's all. He's right there waiting

for you. Would you like to pray together?"

"No," Tam said, feeling awkward.

"Then I'll pray for you," Hope said. "I'll keep on praying till I know you've found Him."

Tam didn't answer. She didn't like the idea of being prayed for. It made her uncomfortable. The conversation had gone too far.

After that she tended to avoid Hope. Too many feelings were out in the open and Tam needed space to think in. The others felt that way too. They were much less social than usual. Even Mack kept his distance, sensitive to feelings unexpressed, although his employees would never believe he cared about anything but groceries.

Around eight Stewart came in. He had never come early before, so immediately Tam knew something was wrong.

"Get your things," he said. "I'll tell Mack you're leaving."

In the car, Tam said, "What's the matter?"

"Your dad's had another stroke," Stewart said. "He'll be all right, we think, although it's too soon to tell. We knew you'd want to be with him."

Tam wanted to scream and cry and kick. Instead she sat calmly listening to the details and asking sensible questions. She might have been discussing a register error for all the emotion she showed on the surface.

Stewart talked quietly as he drove to the hospital, explaining the details and re-explaining when she asked him the same questions again and again.

Dad had been watching the bird feeder when the squirrels came after the sunflower seeds. Mrs. Warren saw him charge off the porch with a broom, flailing at the squirrels and shouting. Then he dropped the broom and clutched at the arm which had held it and which now hung lifeless by his side. He leaned against the pole.

Mrs. Warren ran to catch him, shouting for Luke as she ran. Luke carried him into the house and made him comfortable while Mrs. Warren called the ambulance and sent Stewart to Food Mart. They would stay with him, Stewart reassured Tam, all the way to the hospital, and were probably there already.

Luke, Tam thought, and was grateful. *Luke could take care of things. He and Mrs. Warren were as good as you could get in emergencies.*

At the end of the third telling, Stewart pulled up to the emergency entrance. Tam jumped out, leaving him to park the car.

I know this place, she thought, hesitating at the uninhabited information desk. *This is the place that took my mother and the place where my father left his career.* She shuddered involuntarily. She looked anxiously around the empty area and wondered where everyone was.

Looking for somebody, anybody, who knew where her father was, Tam dashed past the desk to the waiting room and into Mrs. Warren's arms.

"It's all right," Mrs. Warren crooned. "It's all right. He's in there and the doctor is with him."

"How is he?" Tam asked.

"We don't know yet. We'll have to wait for the doctor's report. Luke's with him. They wanted him to wait out here but he insisted on seeing that they took your dad immediately."

Luke could do that, Tam thought. *If I tried it they would flick me away like a gnat, but it's hard to flick him away.*

A nurse came to get Tam then, to ask questions for those

papers they always fill out. By the time the blanks were filled in, Stewart was there, and Luke, and there was nothing at all to do.

Except pray, Mrs. Warren reminded Tam. As the four linked hands in the waiting room, Tam felt the strength of their faith stand strong around her. Tam's own faith was a blade of grass in high wind, but these friends had firmness of faith that shielded that little blade of grass so it stood in the storm.

They settled in to wait. How long was it before the doctor came out? Tam couldn't guess. It might have been an hour and a half, which is what the chrome-rimmed clock above the door said, or it might have been ten hours, which is what her heart said. She and Luke rose to meet the doctor.

Doctor Thomas said, "He's had another stroke, but it's too early to assess the damage with any degree of accuracy. That will take several days. It would be my guess that the damage is less severe than the damage he suffered from the last stroke."

They would have to keep him under observation until they were reasonably certain there would be no immediate recurrence and his condition was stable. Then it was vital that therapy begin as soon as possible to help him regain use of his right side.

He was conscious, but extremely tired. Tam might see him before they took him up to Intensive Care, but only for a few minutes and only if she took care not to worry him.

She promised.

Lying on the gurney, hair and skin gray against the white sheet, he looked smaller than Tam remembered. More fragile.

She took his "good" hand and held it with steady

pressure. "Doc Thomas says you're going to be okay," she said. "You caused a fuss, but it's all right now. I'll stay with you tonight. I won't go home until the sun comes up. I'll be right here. Okay?"

He tried to smile again and nodded and she knew it mattered to him that she would be there. He waved a wobbly good-bye as the orderlies wheeled him off to the intensive care unit.

"I'm going to stay," she told her friends. "He'll feel better knowing I'm here with him. You go on home."

They offered to stay, to sit with her, to bring supper, to get coffee. At last they agreed to go, leaving Tam in the glass-fronted ICU lounge, waiting alone for the sun to rise.

ten

At two a.m. the ICU lounge of Graham Memorial Hospital was hollow-quiet. Aside from the occasional squeak of foam rubber soles passing by on polished floors and the regular click of the wall clock hand pouncing on the next minute, her own breathing was the only sound Tam heard.

The ancient magazines couldn't interest her in making Christmas wreaths of bread wrappers and Easter baskets of empty bleach bottles, not in August. The drinking fountain down the hall produced warm, iron-flavored fountain water, but she made several trips to taste it, not because she was thirsty, but because there was nothing else to do. When Dad was here last time, Tam's mother had knitted a whole sweater while she waited. I *should have learned how to knit,* Tam thought.

Tam's feet were cold in their sneakers. She pulled them up under her on the green plastic sofa. Air conditioning set for many visitors overcooled the deserted room. She curled into a ball, conserving the little warmth her lean body produced, and tried to go to sleep.

She wished she were not alone.

At six-thirty, visitors would be allowed to enter to sit with patients as they breakfasted. The sign on the door said so, but it didn't say that breakfast would probably be intravenous. Four and a half hours wasn't so long, Tam thought.

But she wished she were not alone.

She twisted into another position, laying her cheek

151

against the back of the sofa. Maybe this way she would sleep.

She couldn't.

Dad was all right. He had to be. She refused to think of any other possibility. Concentrate on something else. Painted silk. She wondered if anybody would buy. Luke said they would. . .Luke said. . .

Think about work. Mack had let her go when Stewart came. That was nice of him. Tam would thank him tomorrow. . .today. . .when she went to work. Mack was nice about Barbara too. He told Barb straight what the deal was and why he was angry, and he did it without meanness. Some people can't do that. Everything's personal with them. Not Mack. He was willing to give Barb another chance. Barb couldn't ask more than that.

Of course, he wouldn't have been so generous if I hadn't promised to pay, thought Tam, *and I wouldn't have thought of it if Hope hadn't made me feel I should do something. Hope's as beautiful inside as she is outside,* she thought. *Like Stewart.*

Barb had apologized and had even hinted she might go to church. That was a change.

Luke should paint that, Tam thought. *He painted his own change so clearly that she could feel it. He should paint a change for Barb. Or for me.*

Tam longed for the peace reflected in Luke's work. She wanted what he had found and what Hope and Stewart and Mrs. Warren had.

Just ask, Hope had said, But. . .

"I thought you might want some company," said a deep voice from the doorway.

"Luke!"

"I can't work tonight anyway. Might as well come sit with you a while. Brought you a hamburger and a chocolate shake from Megabeef." He held out a little white bag.

"Thanks," Tam said. "I didn't know I was so hungry." She took a long drink of the shake and shivered. "Delicious," she said.

"Cold," he said, and left the room.

In a few minutes he was back with a blanket and a pillow, both welcome.

"Thank you," she said again, wondering where he had gotten them. "I say that to you pretty often. You always seem to be there when I need you."

"Yes," he said, simply. "Any news?"

"No."

He strode directly to and through the extra wide doors labeled "Authorized Personnel Only." Soon he was back with the news that Dad was sleeping and was no worse. Knowing this was a great relief, and Tam wondered why she hadn't thought of opening those doors to ask.

"How did you know to do that?" she asked.

"Do what?"

"Go in there and find out how Dad is," she said.

He shrugged. "One hospital is pretty much like another. If you want something, you have to ask for it."

"You should like Hope," she said.

"I don't understand," Luke said.

"Never mind," she mumbled. "It's hard to explain."

Without another word he sat next to her, filling the entire middle of the sofa and adding a turpentine tang to the air. He pulled off her sneakers, tucked the blanket around and under her cold feet, then pulled the wrapped feet onto his lap, where he massaged them firmly, warmly with one hand, as if he massaged her feet every night.

"Now explain," he said. "And take your time. We have all night."

So she told him about wanting to study art, about giving up that dream and settling for Food Mart. She told him about losing Robert and Mother, about fears of losing Dad, about being alone, and about trying to be tough when she wasn't tough at all.

He listened.

She poured out her whole heart to him, telling secrets she had hidden in her heart for years.

She hesitated.

He waited.

Then she told him about the Road to Emmaus and how she wanted whatever it was he and Stewart and Mrs. Warren and Hope had. "You know how to find it," she said, sitting straight up, dropping feet and blanket to the floor. "I saw it in your paintings. Hope said to just ask, but it isn't so easy."

"No," he said, almost smiling, "not for someone as stubborn as you are. It's hard to ask and you have to do it yourself, but you only have to ask once."

Luke prayed with her, supporting her with his strong faith as he had supported her with his strong arms another night when she was lost, until Tam could ask for the peace she wanted.

Then, Luke talked quietly of the changes in his own life, letting Tam hear the hurt under his gruffness. As he spoke, she relaxed, safe with him, and when he lapsed into silence, she fell asleep against his shoulder.

He pulled her awake when the pink-smocked volunteer

arrived at six-fifteen to make coffee and sit at the desk for visiting hour. Other visitors came in and Tam had barely enough time to splash water on her face and comb her hair before time to go in.

"Thank you, Luke," Tam said, again, and he nodded.

Dad looked better, but was docile, a sure sign he was not feeling well.

Luke took Tam home by way of the diner on the bypass, where he fed her pancakes and sausage. She said she wasn't hungry at all but she ate the whole stack.

"You need some sleep in your own bed," he said.

He pulled the beat-up van behind Stewart's car quietly, letting the neighborhood sleep, and eased out of his door, not quite shutting it. Tam eased out on her side, opening her own door. This was not Stewart.

"Wait," he whispered.

He let himself in Mrs. Warren's kitchen door and in a moment or two he returned with one of his canvasses, the one that reminded Tam of the Road to Emmaus.

"Thank y. . ."

He put his fingers over her lips before she could finish it. He shook his head. She nodded and he smiled.

In the deserted house she put Luke's painting on the bookcase, where she could see it from her pillow. She lay there looking at the picture, allowing herself to wander down that road again. She heard the stream and felt the dust beneath her feet. Tall cedars swayed on the other side. She was alone on the Road to Emmaus.

The Stranger waited ahead. She didn't recognized Him, but she welcomed His company. They talked and she understood things she had never understood before and felt a peace she had not known. At the bend in the road He turned toward her and she suddenly knew Him. Jesus.

In peace and safety she slept soundly through the morning.

The phone woke her, cutting through her sleep. The hospital? She jumped up and ran to answer.

"Hello? Tam?" Mack said.

Tam exhaled in relief. She hadn't given Food Mart a thought. Now she did. She had to get to work.

"Tam? Are you there?"

"I'm here," she said. "It's a good thing you called. I might have slept through my shift."

"That's why I'm calling. Would you like to change to days until your father gets out of the hospital? Then you could see him at visiting hours."

Tam hadn't thought of that. Unless she missed work, she could see Dad only at breakfast. Changing shifts would solve that problem.

Mack assured her she could change back to evenings as soon as Dad was better. "Come in at seven tomorrow morning. You can make this day up next week."

Tam said, "Thanks, Mack. I appreciate it. It's kind of you to offer."

Mack laughed. "I don't know how kind it is. Luke says if I want to keep you, it's the only sensible thing to do."

"Luke says?" Tam echoed.

"Yeah, Luke," said Mack. "He stopped by a few minutes ago. Nice guy."

"Yes." What else could she say about a man who was everywhere in her life?

She went back to bed, closed her eyes, and the phone rang again. Stewart. Luke said her schedule was changed and she shouldn't worry about getting to the hospital for evening visiting hours. Stewart would take her.

It was useless to try to get more sleep. She might as well get dressed.

Before she was finished with her hair, Barb called to find out how Dad was and to offer to work her Wednesday shift if Tam needed to take the time off. Tam was explaining the shift change when Mrs. Warren knocked at the back door with two plates of lunch.

Mrs. Warren listened to the conversation while she set the table. She wouldn't have considered eavesdropping, but if someone carried on a conversation where she could hear easily, she naturally assumed it was for her ears too.

When Tam hung up, Mrs. Warren said that since Tam's schedule was changed, they could go to the hospital together at three. Mrs. Warren stayed to eat and to chat a while before she left. That's when Tam noticed how quiet the house was.

She turned the radio on. It helped.

To get away from the strangeness of the house, she went outside to the backyard. Butterflies flickered about in the sunlight above the weeds, the butterfly garden. She hadn't taken time to watch them before, but now she saw that they truly were as lovely as flowers. "Flowers that fly," Luke had called them, quoting some poet.

One squirrel scrabbled in the bird feeder for seeds that weren't there. *I'd better fill that thing for Dad,* she thought. *I know he'll ask.*

She wondered if he could ask, could say those words, or if they were back to the beginning of those speech exercises again. Poor Dad. How much had he lost this time?

The squirrel scurried down the pole. *He's lucky I'm not*

chasing him with the broom the way Dad did, Tam thought. *It would be funny if it weren't so sad,* she thought. She'd never known Dad to do such a thing before the first stroke.

In the living room, she put Dad's corner to rights, setting his chess board, ready for him to come home to.

Alone in the house.

Luke had said she would never be alone again. She looked at Luke's painting, "The Road to Emmaus," and knew as she had known the night before that when she traveled that road, Jesus would talk with her. She was not alone.

With Mrs. Warren she visited Dad, who was in good spirits. His language seemed no more scrambled than it had been before. His right arm didn't work yet, but the therapist already had been there and Dad seemed hopeful. His right leg was affected too, but it seemed improved already. Tam could see for herself that his face was more mobile.

Tam knew that most recovery takes place very soon. If damage is not reversed within the first few days after what doctors insist on referring to as a "neurological accident," the damage may be permanent.

"Neurological accident"—the term made a stroke sound like some little error to avoid by being careful. It didn't seem that minor when the accident happened to a real person.

"He looks pretty good," said Mrs. Warren on the way home, and Tam agreed.

That night Dad was tired so Tam didn't stay long. Stewart stopped in for a few minutes and said Luke would be in at breakfast. Dad was pleased with that. He and Luke had grown close.

Dad liked Stewart, too, but it wasn't the same relationship. With Stewart he talked business and joked around. With Luke he played chess and talked of birds. Tam wondered what else they discussed.

After the visit Tam was too tired to accept Stewart's offer of supper. Besides, she had to get up early for work. She was also too tired to make polite objections when Stewart announced that he would drive her for visiting hours every night and that she should plan on supper with him the next night.

She went to bed just after dark and fell asleep watching Luke's attic light.

The next day went fine after she pulled herself out of bed at six. She had forgotten how early six was. She didn't know the day crew, but they were friendly and easy to work with.

When she punched out at three, she halfway expected Stewart to be waiting. Of course he wasn't. He was at work. Besides, there was no reason to drive her home in the daylight. Instead, she went to the hospital on the bus and would ride home with Mrs. Warren.

That routine lasted for the first week. After that, Dad was moved out of ICU and into a regular room with one o'clock visiting hours, and that was hopeless for Tam. She went at seven with Stewart and left the early afternoon to Mrs. Warren, who usually brought one of Dad's friends, like Mrs. Ellis from the library.

Stewart said Luke had breakfast with Dad every morning, helped Dad eat, and kept him company. Tam didn't see Luke at all. She left the house in the morning after Luke had gone and was at the hospital when he came home. She knew he was working in the attic; she saw his light. Otherwise, he might have vanished, as far as she was concerned.

When did he sleep?

She missed working with Hope and Vickie and Barbara, but they checked in when she checked out, so they stayed in contact. The only person she spent time with was Stewart. They spent hours together in those two weeks. Once she stopped fearing Dad would die and saw he would regain most of the use of his stricken right side, she settled comfortably into a new pattern.

In many ways it was the most normal life she'd had since school. She rose in the morning with the rest of the world and went to work when they did. She came home in daylight and went to bed at ten. It was so wonderfully, blessedly normal.

Stewart was always there. She never quite got used to his dash and glamour. She had difficulty believing he chose her to spend his evenings with, but he did.

They ate out, everywhere. She never knew what she was going to eat when she ate with him. She tried Ravioli con Pesto, which turned out to be fried ravioli in a green, creamy sauce. It tasted pretty good, once she got past the color.

Sauerbraten mit Spaetzle at the Alpine Inn wasn't bad. She could have eaten twice as much spaetzle and half as much sauerbraten, but she didn't know that when he ordered it.

The Acropolis had both best and worst. Moussaka, with eggplant and olive oil, was the worst, but Baklava had to be the world's best dessert.

At Szechuan Blossom, Tam thought she'd have Chicken

Chow Mein or Chop Suey, the only things she recognized. Stewart ordered Sesame Chicken instead, and Beef with Orange Sauce. At his insistence, she tried both. The beef set her mouth afire. Stewart said, too late, that she wasn't supposed to eat the black bean things. She had most of the chicken.

Tandoori Chicken from India Palace was great, and of course she liked the Chimichangas at El Rancho, though she preferred tacos.

Empton didn't offer these foreign foods. Empton had hamburgers and fried chicken. Stewart found these strange foods by driving all over Indianapolis. Her mother had always said Tam left enough food on her plate to feed the starving children of China, so Tam pictured the children of other countries eating the same things she did, like peanut butter. Stewart fed Tam foods she never knew existed.

Mrs. Warren was shocked when she discovered that Tam was wearing her same old cotton skirts to all these places and insisted Tam borrow two of her summer dresses. Not silk, these were fresh cottons which were newer and finer than Tam's old clothes. Mrs. Warren didn't like the looks of Tam's shoes either, but Tam promised to invest in some new ones soon. Until then the old ones would be fine. Tam was glad Mrs. Warren hadn't seen her underwear. It was spotless, clean, of course, but worn-out.

Stewart was too gentlemanly to complain about her clothes. He just complimented her extravagantly when she wore something different. Tam got the idea.

It was a busy two weeks. Every night they took their stomachs to another country, another adventure. For Tam, who hadn't been anywhere for years, each night was a party.

Several times she tried to tell Dad what fun they had and where they had been and how nice Stewart was to her, but it seemed to irritate him. She knew she wasn't doing anything he could disapprove of, but because he seemed upset by it, she stopped telling him unless he asked.

Stewart was the most exciting date a girl could have—considerate, kind, and lots of fun. He probably knew that; Tam didn't see how he could miss it.

He also knew she was nervous. He didn't rush her into passionate embraces. He kissed her once or twice every night, carefully and gently, with enormous tenderness. That was all, except that now and then he took her hand and turned on charm so thick she couldn't look at him. Or he slid his arm around her shoulders and ruffled her hair at the back of her neck while they waited in a booth for their orders.

Initially these touches intimidated her and she had to steel herself against pulling away. Gradually she became accustomed to it, more or less. This was Stewart, after all; kind, good Stewart.

The one place she didn't go with Stewart, although she wanted to, was church. With her new schedule, she missed church entirely. She wanted to worship with others and lose herself in the service as Hope did. She understood why some people refused to work on Sundays, but she needed the work. For now, she had to rely on her own prayer.

Stewart brought messages from people at church who asked how Dad was, and he repeated as much of the services as he could remember, so Tam didn't lose out entirely. Hope said she and Stewart particularly enjoyed the choir that first Sunday and that she was sorry there wasn't a recording of it so Tam could hear it.

Other than missing church and running back and forth to Graham Memorial, the days were pleasant. Occasionally Tam would catch herself wishing they would go on forever, but she dared not get accustomed to this life as she had gotten accustomed to those rides home from work. One day it would stop. She must be ready to accept that.

By the middle of the second week, however, she was deep into the routine and enjoying every second of it. It was fun and she welcomed fun and laughter. She reveled in the admiring glances Stewart drew from other girls and smiled to think that he was with her. If things had gone on that way, exactly that way, she would have been content.

Perhaps she should have seen what would happen, but she didn't. She wouldn't have believed it if she had. She hadn't believed Barb either, when she said Stewart was interested in her. So, for Tam, what happened was a surprise.

The Madrid, a Spanish restaurant where they had gone for Paella, was on the far side of Indianapolis, and the cook had given extra time to preparing their dinner, so they came in later than usual that next Saturday night.

Stewart turned off the engine and Tam waited for him to kiss her two or three times and take her to her door, as he always did.

He didn't.

He sat for a long moment and then, without speaking, reached for her hand. He held it against the cool leather of the seat, absently stroking the back of her hand with his thumb.

What's wrong? she wondered. Then she knew this was the night the party would end. He was trying to find a kind way to tell her he was not going to take her out any more, that the romance was over but that they could remain friends. He was trying not to hurt her feelings.

Well, all right, she could cope with that. She'd been expecting it. She'd make it easy for both of them. She'd thank him for all the fun and they would part friends.

"Tam," he began, and she braced herself as he looked straight at her, "Tam, I. . . Oh, I'm not very good at this."

Releasing her hand, he dug in his blazer pocket and fumbled out a little square box. "Open it," he said.

Inside, glittering against blue velvet, was a breathtaking diamond ring.

"Will you marry me, Tam?" He took the ring from the box and slipped it on her finger, where it glittered in the moonlight.

"It's beautiful," she breathed.

"So are you," he whispered. "You and I can have a good life together."

She fluttered her fingers slowly, watching the moonlight play on the diamond. It dazzled her. Moonlight, handsome man, diamond—a dream, perfect. Almost. She said, carefully, "You haven't said you love me."

He looked away and then back. "If you want me to say it I will, but. . . Look. I like you better than any other girl I've known, and I think you like me. That's enough for now. Love will come, in time. Until then, let me share my life with you. Let me give you things, beautiful things. We can go places, do things. You can study interior decorating, if you like. You can fill my life with home and children and laughter. You can make me very happy, and I promise to try to make you happy too. Please say yes."

Slowly, very slowly, still watching it sparkle, she drew the ring from her finger and held it out to him. He didn't take it. She opened his hand, laid it on his palm, and closed his hand over it.

"I can't," she said. "I know this has to be the dumbest thing I ever did in my life, but I can't. You're a wonderful man and you'd be a wonderful husband, but I can't marry you."

"Think it over," he said, trying to give back the ring.

She said, "I don't have to. I know I can't. I'm sorry."

"If you change your mind, the ring will still be here," he said. "I can wait. I know we're right for each other. Luke says you're one girl in a million and that if I know what's good for me, I'll marry you fast. Luke says you. . ."

"Luke says?" Tam's eyes opened wide and she sat straight up. "Luke says?" she repeated. "What does Luke have to say about whether or not you should marry me?"

Stewart swallowed. "Nothing. . . not exactly. He just said he thought you were the girl I needed. That's all."

"So, you're proposing to me because Luke told you to," she said, in dangerous, measured tones.

"It isn't like that," Stewart protested. "Not exactly. I wanted to ask you. I did. I do. Luke says. . ."

"Luke says!" she fumed. "Always 'Luke says.' All I ever hear is 'Luke says.'" Her voice was gaining volume as her temper rose. "Can't anybody make a move unless Luke says? Can't you even marry without his permission? Do you let him tell you what to think and who to love? That's crazy! It's disgusting!"

Her anger mounted and she gave words to it. "You tell Luke to mind his own business. You tell him I don't want to hear another thing he says. I don't care what he says. You tell him the next time he wants to arrange my life he needs to ask me first. You tell him. . ."

"I won't *have* to tell him if you shout any louder," said Stewart.

"Good! Then I'll shout!"

She climbed out of the car and stood beneath the attic window. "Luke? Luke!" she shouted. "Do you hear me?"

"I hear you," he growled from the window. "Everybody in the neighborhood hears you."

"Fine," she called. "That's just fine. Let them all hear that I am sick and tired of your meddling in my life. Who do you think you are to decide who I should marry? Who asked you? How dare you! Mind your own business. Leave Me Alone!"

No answer. Her words died on the night air. He stood looking down at her, silent. She glared up at him. Silence.

She huffed back to the car.

"I'm sorry," she said to Stewart. "It's not your fault. You should be glad you're not marrying me."

She slammed the car door, leaving him sitting stunned behind the wheel. She slammed the kitchen door behind her. When she looked back, Luke was still standing at the attic window.

"How dare he," she muttered under her breath. "How dare Luke try to push his friend into marrying me. Who does he think he is?"

She stamped through the dark house to her bedroom and glared at the angry reflection in the mirror. How humiliating, she thought. How perfectly wretched to be pushed at some nice guy like Stewart. Stewart probably would have done it, too, married her—just because Luke said he should. How awful. How depressing.

I'll never be able to face Stewart again, she thought. *Not now. Not after I sat there and let him propose to me like that. He and I both know he doesn't love me. And I don't love him either.*

He probably thought I'd jump at the chance to get married, especially to him. Me, the girl with nobody and nothing, and I turned him down. He must have been surprised. He should have been stunned, she thought, and humphed a little sound of disgust.

Well, I told him. . . him and his friend Luke. I really told them.

Her stomach turned over. She had refused a diamond ring and a storybook future from the nicest man she had ever gone out with. She had stood out there in the driveway and shouted angry words at his friend Luke, who had been there every time she needed a friend, who had done nothing but good for her.

Luke! Unless he was meddling in her life, she never saw him. He never visited unless she was away. He avoided her and devoted his attention to Hope. He grouched at Tam, looked through her, looked into her heart. He popped in and out of her life, understanding and ignoring her in turns, lifting her up, and dropping her into Stewart's hands.

Luke, she cried inside. *How could you do this to me?*
"Luke. . ." she cried aloud.

Then the anger and dismay welled up and overflowed,

falling in tears and shaking her in great gulping sobs that she buried in her pillow.

eleven

"Stupid," said Barb.

Tam hadn't intended to tell her, but every time they met Barb asked when Stewart was going to propose. Tam always laughed it off. The day after the driveway disaster, Tam didn't laugh. At first she didn't answer at all, and then the whole story was out.

"Stupid," repeated Barb. "You should have grabbed that diamond quick. I would have. If Stewart needs a wife, send him to me. I'll marry him."

"But we're not in love," Tam protested.

"Listen," Barb said. "Do you know how many married couples don't even like each other? Stewart likes you and you like him. That's more than most people get. He didn't lie, either. He could have lied and said he loves you and you wouldn't have known different until after you were man and wife. Maybe not even then."

"I don't want like," Tam said. "I want love "

"So maybe you'll learn to love each other," Barb said. "It happens."

"No."

Barb persisted. "You'll never have another chance like this. Think it over."

"No."

But she did think it over, walking home in the afternoon sun. *Maybe Barb was right*, she thought. *Only a fool would refuse to marry Stewart.*

Then she was a fool, that's all. In the brightness of day she examined the choice she had made in moonlight and knew it was right. She wished. . . What difference did it make what she wished? With Tam it must be love or nothing.

That was no excuse for her exhibition of bad temper, however. Shouting. Childish. She cringed at the memory of it.

She hoped she didn't run into any neighbors. They were bound to have heard, especially Mrs. Warren.

Childish. Embarrassing.

Tam owed Stewart an apology. She had apologized last night, but she did it in anger. He deserved better.

And Luke. . . She didn't know about Luke. She was angry with him last night and angry today. Thinking about him standing silent made her furious all over again. Surely she was right to tell him to mind his own business. Surely she was entitled to be angry.

Of course I was, she thought, *but did I have to tell the entire world?* At the time it felt very satisfying. Now it seemed a bad-tempered over-reaction to Luke's meddling.

So who gave him the right to meddle? Tam did. She welcomed his meddling when he came out in the rain to lift her from the gravel and she was grateful when he roused her father's interest with the bird feeder. She was in the blouse painting business because Luke made Stewart believe she could do it. She'd welcomed Luke at the hospital that night, too. She could never forget that.

What should she do about Luke?

About three minutes after Tam got home, Mrs. Warren tapped on the door and stuck her head in. "I brought some zucchini bread," she said, sitting down at the table. She went directly to the point. "I heard you last night."

"You and the rest of the neighbors," Tam said. "I'm sorry. I behaved like a child having a tantrum. I had no business yelling like that."

"You can yell if you want to," Mrs. Warren said. "You can even keep me awake with your crying. You can *not* expect me to ignore it."

"I didn't realize I was crying so loudly. I should have shut the window."

Mrs. Warren said, "Our houses are very close together. I couldn't help hearing anymore than you could help crying. You might as well tell me about it. I'll find out anyway."

"Stewart asked me to marry him last night," Tam said.

"I know," Mrs. Warren said. "He told me. He also said you turned him down."

"I had to."

"I know," Mrs. Warren said. "Your father and I told Luke it wouldn't work. He didn't ask our opinion, you understand. We just guessed what he was up to. First, Luke insisted that Stewart pick you up after work, which was funny because Luke was the one who worried about your getting home all right.

"Then he wanted me to invite you over after church. That was fine. I love having you and I would have asked you even if he hadn't asked me to. It was his wanting me to that caught my attention. That and the way he made sure Stewart spent every second of the afternoon with you."

"Poor Stewart," Tam put in.

Mrs. Warren was indignant. "Forget that 'Poor Stewart'

nonsense. Stewart's a big boy, and a stubborn big boy at that. If he didn't want to drive you around in that little car of his, he wouldn't. Taking you out to eat at those fancy places was his idea. He wanted to take you out and he enjoyed it. He likes you."

"He told me," Tam said. "But why me? I should think he'd go out with girls more like he is. He could have his choice of pretty girls with college educations and rich clothes and time to spend enjoying themselves."

Mrs. Warren laughed. "He does, honey. Haven't you seen the way Hope looks at him? She'd go out with him in a minute if he'd just say the word, but not as long as she thinks you're in love with him."

"Where did she get the idea I was in love with Stewart?"

"From Luke," Mrs. Warren said. "You must have noticed the way he cuts in when those two get close together. He keeps Hope away from Stewart."

"I thought Luke wanted Hope for himself," Tam said. "He sure spends time looking into those blue eyes of hers."

Mrs. Warren said, "That's not the way it is, believe me. Luke says he doesn't want to get involved with anyone, ever. He must have been terribly hurt when his wife died."

Mrs. Warren paused, then said, "Now tell me why you were crying up a flood."

Tam thought it over. "I'm not sure I understand it myself. I just got so angry all of a sudden."

Tam tried to explain how angry she was with Luke for pushing Stewart at her, and how tired she was of hearing what Luke said, and how humiliated she felt, and how ashamed.

"I'm still angry," she said. "I know I shouldn't be,

but I am."

"So that's how it is," Mrs. Warren said. "I thought so."

"Now what?"

Mrs. Warren shook her head. "You've got a problem, all right. If I were you, I'd pray about it."

Munching warm zucchini bread after Mrs. Warren had gone, Tam knew she was right. She would have to pray for help. For a new Christian with a temper, it would be a real test, but she would do it. She wondered where Jesus would lead.

Good thing I have the zucchini bread, she thought. *After last night I won't be seeing Stewart again. I'll have to make this my supper and get to the bus stop if I want to see Dad.*

A familiar slam of a car door caught her attention. Looking out the window, she saw Stewart. A time to apologize, she thought, and ran out the door.

Stewart came warily toward her. Suddenly she felt foolish and schoolgirlish standing on the steps with half a slice of zucchini bread in her hand. He didn't seem to notice.

"Stewart," she began, "About last night. . ."

"Later," he said. "I want to change out of this hot suit if I'm going to drive you to the hospital."

"You don't have to do that."

He said, "I know." He reached out and took the bread and stuffed it into his mouth. "Thanks," he said with his mouth full, and walked off, leaving her with butter on her fingers.

He's not angry, she thought, in amazement and relief.

In the car she tried to tell him how sorry she was about

the way she acted. "I'll stand out in the driveway and shout that I'm sorry, if it will help," she offered.

He said, "Forget it. I'm sorry about the way I proposed. I'm not very good at asking girls to marry me. I've never done it before."

"It was beautiful," she said. "Saying no was probably the dumbest thing I've ever done."

"Right! I think you should reconsider," he said.

"No, I have and the answer is still no. You're a fine man and I'd be proud to be your wife, but we don't love each other. With me it's all or nothing. Sorry."

"Me too," he said.

They didn't tell Dad. Tam thought he looked surprised to see Stewart with her, and wondered who had told him. Maybe Luke or Mrs. Warren had told him in the afternoon. Or perhaps she was reading more into his look than was there.

The good news was that Dr. Thomas said Dad could go home in two or three days—Monday maybe, or Tuesday.

Monday afternoon would be terrific, Tam said. She'd work day shift on Monday and ask Mack to put her back on evenings for Wednesday. Since Tuesday was her regular day off, that would work out fine.

She left the hospital in better spirits. Dad was coming home. Stewart was still her friend. She had a few problems, mainly Luke, to solve, but she would trust Jesus to show the way.

"I'm glad you're not angry, Stewart," she said, as they drove home.

He laughed. "I can't fight with you. We're business partners. You owe me money and I intend to see that you pay it back."

"I will. I promised," she said. "I shouldn't have tried to start that business."

"Too late," he said. "You have orders to fill." He had orders for a dozen blouses at one store and six at each of two other stores—two dozen blouses—for immediate delivery.

"I don't know where to start," she said, panicking.

"Order blouses from the Indianapolis supplier, get those labels run off, set up a work area. . ." He reeled off instructions.

"Right," she said, biting her thumbnail.

That was Saturday. Tam couldn't do business with suppliers until Monday. At Food Mart she checked out groceries and thought of painting blouses. She punched the time clock and calculated costs of labels and two dozen plain silk blouses. She spoke to customers and pictured them wearing her Butterflies.

Walking home, Tam realized she had completely forgotten to be angry with Luke. Creative work, right when she needed it. *Lucky timing,* she thought. *No, a gift from God. Thank you, Jesus,* she breathed as she walked. *Thank you.*

When Tam said that Dad had been managing her little blouse business and asked if it would be too taxing for him, Dr. Thomas said it was exactly what he needed. Dad was delighted when Tam and Stewart told him about the blouses that night and glowed when they told him they needed his business skills. *Another gift,* Tam thought, and breathed another thank you.

There was to be a special song service after church that night, Stewart said, beginning whenever church let out.

They had time to make it if she wanted to go.

Of course she did. She used to go to those song services when she was in the youth group. The whole gang went to church and always, every Sunday night, met afterward downstairs or in someone's home. When there was a special service, they were automatically part of it. It would be like old times.

Hope sat alone in the fifth row. Tam had seen her outside and had nodded, but Hope looked quickly at Stewart and then away. *Staying away from* him, Tam thought. *I'll fix that.* She led Stewart to Hope's row and slid in next to her. Stewart followed. Then Tam said to Stewart, "Do you mind if I sit on the aisle?" Tam rose and slid past him. Now he was between Hope and her. *Take that, Luke,* she thought, pleased with herself.

Hope was blushing. *She likes him,* Tam thought, startled. *Luke must have known. How dare Luke meddle in other people's lives! Stewart and Hope were perfect together.*

Mr. Moore announced the first hymn and they sang without a leader, harmonizing, moving easily from one favorite melody to another and then another. Sometimes the transition was without break. Other times, a song would end and then, after a moment's quiet, a new song would begin quietly with one person. Those who heard picked up the melody until all joined.

They sang enthusiastically, raising their voices in praise. Then, by unspoken agreement, their selections grew more introspective, until the voices were a prayerful whisper.

Mr. Moore asked if there were requests for prayer. Mrs. Warren, in the back, asked for prayer for Tam and her father. Ben mentioned an unfamiliar name. Other names were mentioned, and then unnamed requests were made by uplifted hands. Tam lifted her hand. She had much to ask. She felt Stewart's arm move as she raised her hand. She would pray for him and for Hope.

After prayer, old Mr. Chartwell rose to thank God for his eighty years and to declare that he would spend his remaining time praising and thanking God. A woman across from Tam rose to say that she was new to the community and had been drawn to the church by the welcoming friendliness of its members. She thanked God for leading her to this place of fellowship.

Amens followed, and then a long silence. "Alleluia" they sang then, and Tam's heart was full. They sang more joyously with each song, and it was time to close. They held hands, all up and down the rows and across the aisles for the final prayer and through the last song, the same song they had sung years ago when Tam was in the youth group: "God Be With You Till We Meet Again," and then they released hands and filed out quietly.

In the aisles some reached out to touch others, to hug, to share, but they didn't speak.

Outside Tam said, "I think I want to walk. I need to keep the silence a while longer." She noticed Hope walking the other direction and said, "Hope has a long walk home, though. She might appreciate a ride."

Stewart looked long at Tam, then nodded and leaned down to kiss her lightly on the forehead before hurrying to catch up with Hope.

She didn't plan to send Stewart after Hope, but when it happened it felt right. She pictured them together—a handsome pair.

Shadows played on the sidewalk beneath the trees on the familiar, friendly street. She strolled slowly, enjoying the soft quiet of the evening. Home was a short walk away. She wanted to make the most of it.

Dad would come home tomorrow; she would no longer have to return to an empty house. They'd begin again. He'd make tea and toast and watch for birds. He'd have a lesson in the morning and no doubt be as difficult as he was before. His temper was part of her life by now and was almost lovable. Her own temper needed work.

In the afternoons he'd watch television and Tam would go to work. At night she'd make tea and tuck him in. They'd go on as they had before, endless days stretching before her in accustomed sameness.

Fine, she thought, *just fine.* Where once she had wriggled and itched under the drabness of her life, she now accepted the routine, but with some important differences.

No longer would she mourn her lost art studies. She would plant lovely gardens on silk and know that her work brought pleasure to the wearers. She'd hum as flowers flowed from her brush, content with creating beauty.

She was finished wishing for Robert. She was glad to have loved him, but she'd no longer resent his leaving.

Life had not passed her by after all. Stewart had shown her kindness and pleasure and had thought highly enough of her to ask her to share his life. She had the consolation of knowing that and of knowing she had made the right decision.

Most of all Tam had found peace. She knew now that she belonged to Jesus and that he would keep her in His care. It made all the difference.

Footsteps and voices sounded behind her. Mrs. Warren was in earnest discussion. The volume seemed to drop as the footsteps grew closer, but it didn't matter. Tam wasn't listening.

Mrs. Warren must have seen Tam, but she did not call out to her. That was good. Tam wanted to be alone and she supposed Mrs. Warren and her companion wanted to continue their private talk, so Tam crossed the street and walked faster, glancing over her shoulder. Mrs. Warren's friend was Luke.

I didn't see Luke in church, Tam thought. *He must have sat in back. As big as he is, it seems impossible that I overlooked him outside. But then, I wasn't looking. He would never bother to avoid me by blending into the background and out of my sight.*

No? Then why don't I ever see him? For a man who lives next door, a huge man, he's nearly invisible.

She'd have to see him one of these days to apologize, but she dreaded it. She was afraid of what he would read in her eyes.

Not tonight, she decided, and locked her kitchen door behind her. The solid knock at her door startled her.

"Who is it?" she called.

"Luke."

She unlocked the door and opened it, but left the screen shut.

He said, "We have some talking to do."

She opened the screen and stepped out on the back porch with him. She was glad it was too dark for him to see her face clearly. They stood next to each other at the railing, staring into the night toward the butterfly garden.

She cleared her throat experimentally. "I have to apologize," she said. "I shouldn't have shouted at you like that. I'm terribly ashamed of myself and I don't blame you if you're angry. I'm sorry, really sorry."

No response came from the tall shadow looming next to her in the shadows.

"Did you hear me?" she said. "I'm trying to apologize."

"I heard you," he growled.

"Then say something," she snapped.

No answer. She went to the door and opened the screen.

"Wait," said the shadow. "Please."

She waited.

His voice was husky and low. "I'm sorry I interfered between you and Stewart. I thought it would work out. I'm sorry I messed it up for you."

Tam said, "You didn't. We're still friends, no thanks to you. How could you dump me in his lap like that? How could you do that to him?"

"I thought you were the best thing that could happen to him," he said. "It wasn't dumping. You have so much to offer and you've had such a hard time. I wanted you to have what you deserve. I thought. . ."

"You thought I'd jump at the chance to marry him," she flared. "You thought I'd be grateful to marry anybody, even a man you pushed into proposing. Well, I'm not desperate enough to marry without love, not even such a fine man as Stewart."

"It wasn't like that," Luke said.

"Sure it was, only your plans didn't work." She was getting angrier.

"You're shouting," he said.

"I don't care," she shouted. Then she said, very quietly, "Yes I do. Sorry. You make me angry."

"I see that," he said. "What you said, about my meddling in your life. Did you mean it? Do you want me to go away?"

"Yes! No. I don't know," she stumbled. "I mean, you've done so much to help me. I don't even know where to begin to thank you. You're there when I need you and I feel safe when you're near, like nothing can hurt me. You understand when I talk to you and sometimes when I don't. I feel. . .close to you. But. . ."

"But?"

"But then, just when I think you're my friend, you vanish. It's like you're ashamed to have anything to do with me," she said. "Or like you hate me."

"I don't hate you. You can't believe I hate you," he said.

She said, "Why not? One minute you're looking at me like you see into my soul and the next minute you act like we're strangers. When I just about get used to the idea that you don't care what happens to me, you show up again and do something so wonderful that it takes my breath away. Then you're gone again. Friends don't act like that."

"I'm sorry," he whispered. "I don't mean to hurt you."

"Well, you did," she said, feeling more miserable how with anger giving way to confusion.

"I know," he said.

They stood in silence, staring. At last she moved to the door. "Luke?"

"Yes?"

"Luke, I. . ."

"I know," he said. "I'm sorry."

He went into the night. She heard his feet on the gravel and then heard Mrs. Warren's door shut. He would be going up to paint, she thought, gone again from her life. This time he wouldn't be back. Their special link was broken.

She entered the dark house, locking the door behind her.

Special link. She hadn't put it into words before, but it had been there. She'd lost it before she knew it existed. Now it was gone and the loss was painful. Painful.

She slipped through the hall to her room and looked up at the attic window. It was dark.

"What's-his-name-the-painter" she had called him before she knew him. She'd thought him gruff and heartless. Now she knew better.

He was solid and strong. He'd been gentle and kind and caring—almost as if he loved her. With him she found understanding that needed no words. She knew him in the furious brush strokes on his canvasses and felt his strength in the way his hands held her. Strong hands....huge arms ...massive chest with his heart beating against her ear.

She shivered with the memory of that night in the rain.

Stop it, she told herself. *You're making a dream of something that means nothing to him. It's not his fault you love him.*

I love him! she thought with astonishment. *I love him. If I had known. . .*

But she hadn't, and now it was too late.

Oh, Luke!

She sank to the bed in tears. "Luke," she cried. "Luke. I didn't know." And she sobbed.

The pounding on the back door didn't stop. Wiping her

tears, she went to answer it.

"Open the door, Tam." ordered Luke. "Open the door right now!"

She opened the door.

He pulled open the screen door and grasped her firmly by the wrist. "Come," he ordered, pulling her out and across the driveway. Mrs. Warren's door was still ajar and he pulled her into the house, though the kitchen, past Mrs. Warren, and up the stairs, across the second floor landing, and up into the attic.

"Stand there," he ordered, "Don't move."

She stood. He flicked the light switch and around her blazed reds and oranges and yellow greens shouting at her in jagged lines of anger. Sorrow spoke in murky amorphous darknesses. Light blues, soft neutrals, and gentle earth tones soothed and softened in peaceful scenes.

He dragged an easel around so she could see what he was working on. "Look," he commanded.

On the easel was a new color, a soft rose-pink, exactly the color of her silk dress. She wiped her eyes to see more clearly. On the canvas, in a rose-pink dress that floated on a light summer breeze, a lovely young woman smiled gently.

Her hair was dark rich brown, almost black, with little traces of white in the front, like Tam's hair, except that in the picture the gray was a sparkle of silver, a diadem. Beneath the graceful hand the lovely young woman had lifted to shade them, her eyes were soft and warm, dreamy.

She looked like someone Tam should know. She looked like. . ."

"Me!" Tam gasped.

"Yes," Luke said angrily. "You."

Tam couldn't take her eyes from the girl in the picture. "It can't be me. She's beautiful."

"It's you," he said, "the night Stewart took you to Chez Raoul. I saw you on the step in your pink silk. The breeze caught the edge of your skirt exactly so."

"But her hair. . ." Tam began.

"Your hair," he corrected. "It's a problem, your hair. I had to do it and redo it to get the silver to sparkle in it the way yours does. But your eyes were easy. They simply appeared there under my hand. . ." His voice trailed off.

They stood silently regarding the picture. Then abruptly he said, "Here. You might as well see the rest of them." In two giant steps he reached the small stack he had kept away from her the last time she was here. Now he set them in the light.

They were Tam. All of them. One was almost a sketch, a face in the dark with a wispy look about it. The next was wildness and hurt, a waif fallen on a background of gravel. In the third she stared with empty eyes that followed the viewer, haunting. In the fourth, a laughing Tam sat at a dinner table. In another, a shabby Tam sat dejected on a step. In one more, the Road to Emmaus loomed above her as she searched it, lost.

Canvas after canvas of Tam, recognizable in both look and spirit. She felt again all the emotions in turn as she moved slowly, deliberately from one to the next and the next. At the end of the row she surveyed the whole group. Together they said more than they did individually.

He had placed them in order. She saw that now. Pretty in the first painting, she was lovely in the third and beautiful in the last several. The colors changed too. Early ones were neutrals with a dash of strong color, like emotions breaking through distance. The last one, on the easel, was in rich, warm, vibrant color, with no neutrality about it. Every brush stroke of cherished love.

Love!

"So now you know," he said at last. "I didn't want you to see them because you understand too much when you look at my work. You see into me. I... I didn't want you to."

"But why?" Tam said to the girl in the portrait.

"Because you deserve better," Luke said behind her. "You should have an easy life with a handsome husband who is steady and solid."

"So you gave me Stewart," she said.

"I tried to, but you wouldn't have him."

"I don't love him."

"I know," he said, and then there was a long silence.

Luke broke it, saying, "I can't love anybody. I can't. I paint pictures by night and cut trees by day. I have nothing to offer—not much money and very little hope of ever having any—no silk dresses and fancy restaurants. I can't even buy you a house."

"I don't need a house," she said.

"If I gave up painting and took a regular job, I could..." Luke began.

She turned to face him and saw his torn look. "No. You couldn't give up painting and still be Luke."

"I tried not to love you," he said.

"I'm glad you failed."

His eyes searched hers and she opened her heart to let him

see inside it. She floated in his deep eyes, drowning.

"Tamara," he whispered hoarsely, and then his huge strong arms folded around her, lifting her until she was almost chin level. "I love you, Tamara."

"I love you, Luke," she whispered, sliding her arms around his neck.

He lowered his lips to hers and kissed her, gently at first, and then with a power born of the love he offered, kissed her until she grew dizzy and pulled back from him. He kissed her again, lightly, and slowly lowered her until she could stand. "Marry me," he said.

"Whatever you say, Luke," she answered, and he bent to kiss her again.

A Letter To Our Readers

Dear Reader:

In order that we might better contribute to your reading enjoyment, we would appreciate your taking a few minutes to respond to the following questions. When completed, please return to the following:

Karen Carroll, Editor
Heartsong Presents
P.O. Box 719
Uhrichsville, Ohio 44683

1. Did you enjoy reading *Design for Love*?
   ☐ Very much. I would like to see more books
      by this author!
   ☐ Moderately
      I would have enjoyed it more if _____

   _____

2. Are you a member of *Heartsong Presents*? Yes   No
   If no, where did you purchase this book? _____

   _____

3. What influenced your decision to purchase
   this book? (Circle those that apply.)

          Cover   Back cover copy

          Title   Friends

          Publicity   Other _____

4. On a scale from 1 (poor) to 10 (superior), please rate the following elements.

    ___Heroine   ___Plot

    ___Hero   ___Inspirational theme

    ___Setting   ___Secondary characters

5. What settings would you like to see covered in *Heartsong Presents* books?

    _____

    _____

6. What are some inspirational themes you would like to see treated in future books?_____

    _____

    _____

7. Would you be interested in reading other *Heartsong Presents* titles?   Yes   No

8. Please circle your age range:

Under 18	18-24	25-34
35-45	46-55	Over 55

9. How many hours per week do you read? _____

Name _____

Occupation _____

Address _____

City _____ State _____ Zip _____

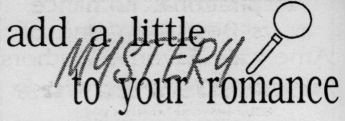

add a little *MYSTERY* to your romance

TWO GREAT INSPIRATIONAL ROMANCES
WITH JUST A TOUCH OF MYSTERY
BY MARLENE J. CHASE

_____*The Other Side of Silence*—Anna Durham finds a purpose for living in the eyes of a needy child and a reason to love in the eyes of a lonely physician...but first the silence of secrets must be broken. HP6 BHSB-07 $2.95.

_____*This Trembling Cup*—A respite on a plush Wisconsin resort may just be the thing for Angie Carlson's burn-out—or just the beginning of a devious plot unraveling and the promise of love. HP5 BHSB-05 $2.95.

Inspirational Romance at its Best from one of America's Favorite Authors!

FOUR HISTORICAL ROMANCES
BY COLLEEN L. REECE

___ *A Torch for Trinity*—When Trinity Mason sacrifices her teaching ambitions for a one-room school, her life—and Will Thatcher's—will never be the same. HP1 BHSB-01 $2.95

___ *Candleshine*-A sequel to *A Torch for Trinity*—With the onslaught of World War II, Candleshine Thatcher dedicates her life to nursing, and then her heart to a brave Marine lieutenant. HP7 BHSB-06 $2.95

___ *Wildflower Harvest*—Ivy Ann and Laurel were often mistaken for each other...was it too late to tell one man the truth? HP2 BHSB-02 $2.95

___ *Desert Rose*-A sequel to *Wildflower Harvest*—When Rose Birchfield falls in love with one of Michael's letters, and then with a cowboy named Mike, no one is more confused than Rose herself. HP8 BHSB-08 $2.95

LOVE A GREAT LOVE STORY?

Introducing Heartsong Presents —
Your Inspirational Book Club

Heartsong Presents Christian romance reader's service will provide you with four never before published romance titles every month! In fact, your books will be mailed to you at the same time advance copies are sent to book reviewers. You'll preview each of these new and unabridged books before they are released to the general public.

These books are filled with the kind of stories you have been longing for—stories of courtship, chivalry, honor, and virtue. Strong characters and riveting plot lines will make you want to read on and on. Romance is not dead, and each of these romantic tales will remind you that Christian faith is still the vital ingredient in an intimate relationship filled with true love and honest devotion.

Sign up today to receive your first set. Send no money now. We'll bill you only $9.97 post-paid with your shipment. Then every month you'll automatically receive the latest four "hot off the press" titles for the same low post-paid price of $9.97. That's a savings of 50% off the $4.95 cover price. When you consider the exaggerated shipping charges of other book clubs, your savings are even greater!

THERE IS NO RISK—you may cancel at any time without obligation. And if you aren't completely satisfied with any selection, return it for an immediate refund.

TO JOIN, just complete the coupon below, mail it today, and get ready for hours of wholesome entertainment.

Now you can curl up, relax, and enjoy some great reading full of the warmhearted spirit of romance.